Stalking Horse

Virvus Jones

ISBN-13: 978-1985855595

To Ryan David

To my parents, Angeline and Charlie who worked hard all their lives to make it possible for me to survive.

To all of the Black people who tried to make politics work for Black people within the system.

To my mentor Pearlie Evans who was fighting the good fight for freedom and justice with her last dying breath.

To my daughters Tishaura, Chelsea and Ida who I love to the moon and back.

To Cory who brought uncompromising love into my life and gave me the confidence to expose my musings and without whom this book would have not been published.

Erynne

A gift for David That
I hope you enjoc

[signature]

CHAPTER 1

It was the beginning of summer and grammar-school graduation day for Teddy "T.C." Chambers, Ronald Jackson, Wiley Fentress, Leonard Marcus, George "Snake" Martin, Demitrius "Meat" Walker and me, Billy Strayhorn.

The question on all our minds: What were we going to do with ourselves now that school was officially out? I was 14, 5'10 tall and weighed 110 pounds; I was the runt of our group.

"So, what are we going to do tonight, fellas?" I asked. "Tomorrow morning, I will be on the highway, going away for the whole summer. We got to do something to celebrate the beginning of summer and our graduation?"

"Who are you bullshitting, Billy?" T.C. barked back at me. "As soon as it gets dark, your little ass will have to go home. And I ain't got your people letting you stay out late just because you graduated from grade school."

"I'm hanging with my raps tonight."

"Yeah, yeah, nigger," he laughed. "We will see! This is T.C. you talkin' to! So don't try that bullshit," he said, sticking his hand out to get fives all around.

"Fuck all that! The proof of the pudding will be in the eating. My question still remains: What are we going to do tonight to celebrate the beginning of summer break?"

"Let's go down to the corner and watch the action at the Panama Lounge," T.C. suggested. TC was a year older than us and was perfect pimp size. We were the same height, but he weighed 130 pounds - 20 pounds heavier and carried it well.

"Man, you know we would get killed if our parents found us anywhere near that place," I responded. "Besides, it's too early."

"When are you going to stop being such a punk?" T.C. snapped. You say one thing and then you punk out. Besides, your cousin owns the place. What do you suggest we do?"

"Let's go up to Richardson Park," I offered. "With school being out, everybody will be there."

"Fuck that!" shouted George, adding his two cents to the conversation. "I am too old to be sitting around a goddamn park. I want to watch some girls — not watch or play with children."

"That's right, Billy," Leonard chorused in, "I want to see some real action tonight. Besides, Jackie Wilson is supposed to be singing at the Panama tonight."

"Yeah, that's right! And since the Panama is owned by your cousin, we can hang out at your house," Ronald said.

"He is not going to be there at 3 o'clock in the afternoon," I said. "Why don't we go up to Richardson Park first? Then when we think the action is about to start at the Panama, we can stop there on the way back?"

"Okay," T.C. said reluctantly, "but if you punk out on us when we get ready to leave the park, you'd better make sure you take your ass to Memphis tomorrow morning — because I am going to talk about you and how you punked out *all* summer long!"

Richardson Park was the summertime hangout for everybody who lived in Petersville's Southend. It was a city-owned municipal park on the corner of Washington and Becket that covered two square blocks.

The park was named after Augusta Richardson, one of the famed Tuskegee Airmen killed in World War II when his plane was shot down over Italy.

The park land had been the site of a military base during the war, but none of the old heads in the neighborhood could tell you with confidence what military mission was conducted there.

In 1952, the military donated the land to the city of Petersville. The city tore down the base and replaced it with a park — for blacks only to placate black leaders who had lodged protests about segregation in the city's municipal parks.

In 1951, a race riot almost erupted at the city's whites-only swimming pool in Randolph Park. Randolph Park was located on the edge of Southend and although Randolph Park was a municipally tax-supported park, blacks were not allowed to use the swimming pool or tennis courts. Fearing friction between blacks and whites would continue and possibly worsen, the white city officials decided to build a park with a swimming pool for blacks.

When we got to the park, it looked like a neighborhood celebration was going on: There were several pick-up basketball games going on, a softball game on the baseball diamond and a noisy crap game at the pavilion.

"Why don't we get the winners for the next basketball game?" I suggested.

"Aw, fuck that," T.C. muttered. "Y'all can do that if you want. I feel lucky. I'm going to shoot some craps."

3

"That's stupid," I said and knew immediately I had fucked up.

It was true, T.C. was my friend, but the one thing you could not do was call him stupid.

Ron, George, Wiley, Leonard, Meat and I were all going to high school and would be in a regular high school program. However, T.C. had been classified and enrolled in a program called "terminal education." I forgot that T.C. was in the program. He did not come to the graduation luncheon because he was ashamed of being in the program.

The designation "terminal ed" was the most awful thing you could be called in school. State law required that a person attend elementary school until age 16. If he did not meet the requirements to graduate from the eighth grade, he was sent to high school and assigned to this program.

Students in the program were allowed to attend only two years of high school. An exception could be made if the student was re-tested and made a minimum score on the Iowa Basic Skills Standardized Test.

T.C., as many black kids, was in fact smart and he had a lot of street sense, but he did not do well on standardized tests. The Petersville Public Schools, at that time, used a three-track system to classify students entering high school. The fact that I had tested into Track One made what I had said to T.C. two times as bad.

T.C. turned, pointed his finger in my face and shouted. "You think your shit smells better than mine Motherfucker?! But you ain't being smart enough to give me a reason why I shouldn't kick your ass for calling me stupid!"

Ron could see T.C. was pretty pissed. He grabbed him and tried to joke with him.

"Come on, T.C., you know Billy is fucked up. He is book-smart, but you and I both know he wouldn't last five seconds in the streets because he ain't got one ounce of street sense. His momma and daddy think that education will make him and his brothers and sisters better than everybody else. But what they don't know is that whites will see them as just a bunch of highly-educated niggers - no different than you or me or any other nigger."

Ron was 5'9" and was built like a miniature tank but could not constrain T.C. as he pulled away from him and grabbed me by the collar.

"Yeah, but I think this nigger needs to be taught a lesson that all that book-shit don't mean a fucking thing in the streets. I've been pissed off all day and been looking for somebody's ass to kick and it might as well be his!"

T.C. was known to carry a knife, and he was not shy about using it. Thinking that I was about to get cut up, I threw up my hands up and tried to cop a plea.

"I'm sorry man!" I yelled. "I know you won't believe this, but I have a lot of respect for you. I see you as an older brother and I appreciate all the times you have kept niggers from fucking with me."

Hesitating for a minute, T.C. suddenly slapped me on the side of my face with the back of his hand.

"The next time you say something like that to me, I am gonna fuck you up!" he said.

Breathing a sigh of relief, I slowly backed away sideways and walked over to the basketball courts.

Following behind me, Ronald Jackson whispered, "You are one lucky nigger, Billy! T.C. is fucked up when he gets angry, and nothing makes him angrier than someone calling him stupid."

"Yeah, I know man. Thanks for helping."

Although T.C. hung out with us, he was really a young gangster. He had spent some hard time at the Ravenville State Reformatory for assault and truancy. T.C. also had two brothers who were linked to all kinds of criminal activities. Even his mother was suspected of fencing stolen goods from boosters.

T.C. was not a nigger to be fucked with.

While all this was going on, Snake had already secured the winners at the basketball court. A game was just ending when he yelled to us. "Come on, y'all! You niggers want to play or do I have to choose some other guys to play with me?"

"Cool out, Bro!" Wiley yelled back. "You ain't got nowhere to go and there ain't nobody better than us for you to choose!"

At the same time, T.C. was walking toward the pavilion to join the crap game.

After about 20 minutes of playing basketball, we heard loud shouting noises coming from the vicinity of the crap game. We saw T.C. standing and yelling at someone.

Then James Washington, a brother who lived across the street from Ron, ran over to him and shouted, "Your boy T.C. is in real deep shit now! Baby Ray accused him of cheating at craps and hit him with his pistol!"

We all stopped playing and rushed to the pavilion. When we got there, T.C. was bleeding from a gash in his head and screaming at Baby Ray.

"I wasn't cheating and you know it, Baby Ray! You just can't take losing!"

"You ought to just shut up and consider yourself lucky, you little punk-ass motherfucker!" Baby Ray laughed. "I normally

6

don't allow motherfuckers who cheat on me to live and talk about it."

Unimpressed, T.C. continued talking. "That's how you win all the time. When you start losing, you just fake some kind of bullshit like this and take all the money. I'm not gonna let you punk me out of my money."

"Who does this little shithead think he is?" Baby Ray laughed again as he slapped the hands of two other men standing near him. He suddenly started waving his gun around. "I heard you were a little retarded. That's the only reason I haven't popped you with this .38! I don't have a reputation of going around shooting crazy motherfuckers."

Everybody except us laughed loudly. They felt comfortable enough to laugh at what Baby Ray said about T.C. because on the Southend, Baby Ray was *the shit*.

Undaunted, T.C. kept on talking.

"I want my money, man. I won it and you know I didn't cheat. They were YOUR dice!"

The gash on T.C.'s head began to bleed like a gusher. Ronald, fearing T.C. was going to further aggravate Baby Ray, walked over to T.C. and whispered into his ear, "You can't win this fight, man! He's got the ups on you. Come on, let's go."

Ronald took a handkerchief from his pocket and tied it around T.C.'s head in an attempt to stop the bleeding.

Heeding Ron's warning, T.C. started walking away, yelling as he left. "This ain't the end, motherfucker! You ain't got shit to look forward to. Nobody steals from me."

"Go on, little young punk. I'm scared to death. You better take the advice of your little basketball-playing friends. If I didn't know your momma, I wouldn't let you talk to me like that and walk away. I would have popped a cap in your ass. Shit, I must be getting soft in my old age."

"Fuck you!" T.C. yelled back. "Don't do me no favors, motherfucker. It ain't over."

T.C's head was still bleeding as we followed him. We tried to get him to stop so we could help. Ronald was the only person T.C. would let near him.

"T.C., you got to let go of this, man. Baby Ray is not the kind of nigger you want to be fucking with."

"Fuck you too, Ron! This nigger is not going to get away with pistol-whipping me, calling me a thief and taking my money. I was winning big-time. I can't let nobody get away with doing that to me!"

"But what are you gonna do, man? Baby Ray is a full-grown, mean motherfucker. People say he has killed at least 12 niggers. You have got to let this shit go!"

"I gotta go, man. I'm going to go home, but I'll be back."

We had never seen T.C. like this before. Ronald had known T.C. longer than anybody else.

His momma, Mrs. Jackson, and T.C.'s momma, Mrs. Chambers, were from the same small town in Mississippi and had worked together at the Small Arms Plant in Petersville during the war. Ron's mother went back to school and became a teacher.

T.C's mother continued working at the Small Arms Plant. All of his brothers and sisters were just like him: They will fuck you up at the drop of a hat. The neighborhood gossip was that Mrs. Chambers had flipped out after T.C.'s daddy left her.

Baby Ray had no idea what he had done. T.C. was not going to let things end like this.

We all knew it.

CHAPTER 2

It was almost 6 p.m. when the shit ended between T.C. and Baby Ray.

The Panama Lounge was beginning to get crowded. The first wave of people getting an early jump on Friday-night partying were starting to show up.

"What are we gonna do now, y'all?" Snake asked. "Do you think we ought to follow T.C. home to make sure he doesn't do anything stupid?"

I immediately pushed my fist into Snake's chest.

"Don't use that word, man! You just saw how mad that made T.C."

"Yeah, I forgot," Snake chuckled. "He was ready to fuck you up. Scared the cowboy shit out of your ass, didn't he?" Snake got his name from his looks: tall and thin. Snake literally slinked when he walked much like a real snake would do.

"Let's go on down to the corner and watch the action at the Panama Lounge," I said. "We can sit on the steps of my cousin Ella's beauty shop. That way, we can see everything going on."

"I guess so," Snake agreed, "but I'm still worried about T.C. That was the maddest I have ever seen him. I don't believe we have seen the end of this tonight. We all know T.C. is not going to let this shit drop. The way T.C. went off on Billy showed he is just looking for somebody to fuck up. I would be more worried if I were Baby Ray."

"Well, what are we gonna do, y'all?" Wiley asked. "Whatever T.C. does, that's on him. I'm not going to let that fuck up my fun."

"Okay, let's go on down to the corner and check out the action," Snake said. "I got something else to do in about an hour."

"Hmmm, I wonder whose momma's daughter is going to get the shit fucked out of her tonight," I joked. "I don't know how you do it, man. Your mind must be on fucking 100 percent of the time."

"If your mind ain't on fucking 100 percent of the time, your mind is wandering," Snake laughed. We all laughed and continued our trek down to the Panama.

As we walked down Emerson Street to Washington Avenue, we could see that a large crowd had already gathered outside the Panama. People were arriving early to celebrate Cousin Pleas' birthday. Last year it was so crowded, people had to park four blocks away. And with Jackie Wilson in town, it was going to be crowded beyond belief.

Pleas' wife, my cousin Ella, owned a beauty shop across the street from the Panama. It was the best seat in the house for us to be able to see all the action.

And every kind of action you wanted could be found at the Panama. The Panama officially opened at 7:30 a.m. and closed at 1:30 a.m. In reality, it never closed. The legal closing time for bars and restaurants in the city of Petersville was 1:30 a.m. Pleas ran an after-hours gambling operation on the second floor above the Panama. For a fee, the Petersville police looked the other way.

The Panama served as a one-stop shop for all the good, the bad and the ugly that went on in Petersville. It was where the drug dealers, gamblers, boosters and thieves made their connections.

All the local black politicians made sure they came through the Panama at least once a week. In those days, the ward bosses controlled everything; they were officially called ward committeemen. If you needed to get on welfare; if you wanted a job in the local, state or federal government; if you needed help bailing someone out of jail — all you had to do was call your committeeman.

In the Southend, the politicians and the criminals operated their delivery systems right next to each other without anyone seeming to care or think it was unusual. It was difficult for the average neighborhood resident to make any distinctions between the two.

Whatever you got from either of them, you paid for it. Both sold services and products that eased the pain of trying to survive in a racist society. If you got a job or assistance from the ward boss, you paid him a finder's fee. He would also make you pay 1 percent of your wages to his ward's organizations every month. If he asked, you also had to work on every Election Day. As long as you had the job, you owed him.

All this took place under the guise of helping you. If you wanted to open a restaurant or any other type of business, you did not have to go downtown to get the necessary health permits or other licenses. You just needed see your ward committeemen.

The ward boss for Petersville was "Big Jim" Connors. Big Jim — or "Black," as most people called him — had been running things in Petersville as the 9th Ward Democratic

Committeeman since the late 1920s. Up until 1932 he like most other black voters and elected officials were Republicans or as my father used to say, Abraham Lincoln Republicans. Black people voted republican because it was the Republican party that led the fight to get rid of slavery. In 1932 at the beginning of the Great Depression, the Democrats had redeemed themselves with blacks living in the urban northern cities. They formed a coalition of labor, farmers, blacks and Jews who blamed the Republicans for the economic depression. Since 1932, only one republican had been elected mayor.

They called him "Big Jim" for all the obvious reasons. He was 6-foot-4 and weighed at least 400 pounds. They also called him "Black" because his skin was coal-black. The word on the streets was that Black controlled everything that went on in the 9th Ward — legal and illegal.

Black's official line of business was burying people. He owned Connors Mortuary. When he wasn't at the Panama, that's where you could find him. He was also my boy Snake's uncle.

That night, every color and make of Cadillac that General Motors made was double-parked in front of the Panama Lounge. Black people being able to own one of the most expensive cars made was really a testament to racism. There were no black owned new car dealers or black salespeople working at the car dealers. Black people could not even patronize the car dealerships. If you were black and wanted to buy a new car, you had to negotiate the sale with black car brokers who earned a portion of the commission for every new car purchase they brought to a white car salesman. Out of every Cadillac stepped a sister of every shade and skin color that God ever created. It was two days after Mothers' Day, the day the mailman delivered the welfare checks, so everybody had money.

From the front porch of Cousin Ella's beauty shop, we had a bird's-eye view of everything.

Black had taken his usual position at a corner table on the right side of the bar, his back against the wall. Everyone who came through the door paid homage to him. There were those who went to get paid or to pay him. Most of them were paying.

In 1954, most people saw the activities of the 9th Ward as simply the way the system worked, and we thought nothing of it. All of us except Ronald Jackson, who called Black's system nothing more than modern-day slavery.

"It's a damn shame what black people will let whites make us do to each other," Ron suddenly blurted out.

Ron usually was the quietest member of our group — until the issue of politics came up. He always had a book in his back pocket on history or politics. He was the only one of us who read a newspaper every day. Ron and I lived on the same street. Each day he would come over an hour before we left for school to get me and report what was in the paper that morning. He was always reading to me something he had already read. He was especially excited about what he was reading about the Civil Rights Movement.

Ron's father owned a small confectionery across the street from the Panama. He got up at 5 a.m. every morning with his father to help him open up and get ready for the day. The morning paper was delivered at 5:30, so Ron always had a chance to read the paper and knew what was going on before he walked to school with us.

"I knew you couldn't hold it in too much longer, so come on, get it out of your system," I said. "Let's hear how the white man is just fucking us in the ass all the time." The other guys slapped my hands in agreement and laughed.

"I don't know what y'all find so funny," Ron said. "People like Connors don't do anything but rape our communities and rip them off. Nothing in the black community gets done through the government unless he is involved. He is a straw boss, a modern-day plantation overseer that the white power system allows to be the gatekeeper for the distribution of political spoils and government services."

Everybody else in the group was willing to ignore Ron — except George, because Ron was talking about his uncle, his surrogate father. George's parents had been divorced for years, and his father did not pay much attention to him. Whatever father-images George had, he got from Black. Ron's bad-mouthing of George's uncle irritated him.

"Are you finished?" George finally interrupted. "My uncle helps a lot of people in ways you don't know about. If all he was doing was fucking over people — like *you* say — he could never get re-elected."

"How naïve can you be, George?" Ron said. "The election process is a sham. No one ever bucks him and wins. If anyone starts to complain, he gets a visit from one of you uncle's goons — like Baby Ray."

"You are just pissed because your old man couldn't open his grocery store," George returned. "All you're doing is repeating what your daddy says."

There was a brief silence. Ron was sensitive to this issue. He and George were close, but George felt a familial need to defend his uncle. In the Southend, everything was fair when you were defending your family.

Meat jumped in, trying to change the subject.

"Look at the ass on that sister! Goddam! Does she have the booty disease or what? When you finish medical school, Leonard, you are going to have to do something about that!"

"I think some things are better off left alone," Leonard cracked back. "God blessed the black woman with a perfect ass. Well, *most* black women."

We all laughed, including Ron and George. You could tell they both knew this could end up going too far. Our focus had moved back to the Panama where, at a table next to Black's, we saw his enforcer, Baby Ray. He was there to make sure nobody fucked with Black. He also ran a policy book for Black and collected from Black's runners at the Panama.

Dressed in a classic white-silk suit, with black-and-white spectator shoes that contrasted with his shiny black skin and flashy, gold tooth, Baby Ray indeed looked the part of a 1950s gangster.

Everything seemed to be settling in when Ron suddenly pointed down the street.

"Isn't that T.C. coming?"

"Yeah, and I think I see a shotgun in his hand," Wiley said.

"Looks like he plans to continue his fight with Baby Ray. Somebody got to try to stop him. He only listens to you, Ron."

"I don't think I can stop him tonight. Y'all know T.C. When he gets pissed, nobody can talk to him."

By now, T.C. was in front of the Panama on the Elliot Street side, looking through the window at Baby Ray, who did not see him at first. T.C. walked up to the window and started tapping on it to get Baby Ray's attention.

"I want my money!" he yelled through the window at Baby Ray.

"Hey, Baby Ray! Who is that kid in the window yelling at?" Black asked him. "Probably one of those bastard kids of yours that you ain't told nobody about. Sounds like he asking for

15

money. You need to take care of your children, man. He is beginning to disturb the fuck out of me. Would you please go out there and shut him up?" he said, waving his arm, motioning for Baby Ray to go outside.

"I am going to shut his ass up, all right — that little motherfucker!" Baby Ray growled. "I guess that whipping I gave him at the park wasn't enough."

Through the window, I could see Baby Ray getting up from his table, where he had been sitting with two of the finest sisters in the place. He obviously was pissed off by the interruption.

"Where are you going, Baby Ray?" one of the women murmured. "I thought we were going to be with you tonight."

Ignoring her, Baby Ray walked to the front door of the Panama. Suddenly, the people waiting in line to get inside began to back away. It's strange how easily people sense that something is about to happen.

Still wolfing, T.C. was yelling, "I want my money, man! I ain't leaving until I get it!"

Baby Ray — slowly, deliberately walking towards T.C., replied in a very calm, low voice, "Then it looks like you ain't leaving, 'cause all you gonna get from me is a good ass-kicking, nigger. You got one last chance to take your little retarded, wanting-to-be-a-man ass home before I fuck you up!"

"You ain't fucking nobody up tonight, motherfucker!" T.C. yelled, revealing a 20-gauge shotgun.

Baby Ray stopped and started laughing.

"Who are you going to shoot with that gun? It's almost big as you, punk."

Baby Ray pranced slowly around T.C., taunting and yelling at him.

16

"YOU are going to shoot ME? You think you can shoot ME, nigger? I eat punk-ass niggers like you for breakfast!"

"That is EXACTLY what I am going to do if you don't give me my money," T.C. yelled back.

By this time, the people inside the bar were starting to gather outside to see what was going on. The scene had also gotten the attention of Black and my cousin Pleas.

Black hollered at Baby Ray, "I thought you were going to take care of that kid! You need some help?"

"Man, I wish you niggers would freeze this shit and take this action someplace else," Pleas yelled. "I don't give a fuck about who did what to whom or who shot John. I'm trying to run a business, and y'all got people looking at y'all — and not buying no whiskey. I don't want no shit tonight, Baby Ray. Your job is to keep shit from happening on this corner — not starting it."

Baby Ray was still taunting T.C.

"Shoot me nigger! You so bad, shoot me! I'm gonna cut your ass up and down this street tonight. The only way you gonna be able to avoid it — is shoot me. But I don't think you got the balls to shoot nobody."

A strange look came over T.C.'s face that only those of us who knew him could recognize. The five of us knew T.C. was serious.

"I'm going to tell you this for the last time: Give me my money, Baby Ray," he said.

Baby Ray continued to laugh. He even turned his back on T.C. and did not see the other finger slowly slip down to the trigger of the shotgun.

A loud blast rang out. Then another.

17

The close-range force of the shotgun sent Baby Ray's body sailing through the front window of the Panama Lounge and his body landed on top of Black's table.

Blood covered his chest and stomach like a red vest. Everyone scattered. Women screamed. In the confusion, Ron grabbed the gun from T.C. and told him to leave.

For the first time that day, T.C. did what Ron told him to do — but it was too late.

T.C. went home but was arrested that night.

The police never found the gun.

Black tried hard to get T.C. charged with murder, but T.C.'s status as a juvenile kept him from going to prison. He was sentenced to Ravenville Reformatory School until he was 21.

Ron, myself, Snake and Meat got permission to visit T.C. at the juvenile detention center which, while not a jail, is a gruesome-looking place. The conditions reminded me of a scene in a Dickens novel.

We visited T.C. on a Sunday afternoon. We brought a "care package" that my mother and the rest of our parents had put together. Because even though our parents did not approve of what T.C. did, they understood why. Ron's father was the most supportive. He blamed it on Connors and the environment created by the white power struggle.

We all rode up with T.C.'s mother. Mrs. Chambers expressed her gratitude to us for supporting T.C. She had deep lines in her face that showed the stress she had experienced trying to raise three boys by herself.

T.C. had committed a capital crime, so he was segregated from the rest of the detainees. Actually, this was good because it allowed us all to get a chance to talk to him face-to-face.

"What's up, my man?" Ron said, reaching out his hand and slapping T.C.'s. "I left you a care package up front. Some Big Time candy bars and oatmeal cookies from Popich's Delicatessen. Billy, Snake and Meat are in the visitor's waiting room. We all came up to see how you doing."

"That means you brought the guards a care package!" T.C. said. "It took my mother six months to catch onto the scam. The guards will come to my cell when you leave and tell me about the package. If I say they can have it, they will do me a favor like letting you see me without a guard being present. I am really surprised that the other fellows came up, especially Billy. I always use to give him a hard time."

"Hey man you are our friend. Billy knew he was wrong. He feels guilty thinking what he said might have been partly his fault. He is mad at himself for what he said and thinks what he said could have contributed to you being in the mood you were in. Your mom said you were sentenced to stay here until you are 21," Ron said. "That is really fucked up."

"Yeah, it is," T.C. sighed, "but it could have been worse. Black was trying to get me a life sentence. Baby Ray was his boy. The judge told me I could petition the court to get out when I'm 18 — if I'm a "good boy." There is one good thing about being in here: I don't have to do that terminal-education thing. I will be able to take regular high-school courses. When I see Billy, I'll tell him that he actually did me a favor if he thinks he was partially responsible for what I did to Baby Ray," T.C. said laughing and slapping my hand.

I was next to go into the prisoner visitor area. I was startled when I reached out to give T.C. five, he grabbed my hand and pulled me to him and gave me a hug. This was so out of character for him and me because brothers from our neighborhood don't embrace. I should have known it was T.C. way of making a point. As he hugged me he whispered in my ear, "Thanks for pissing me off so I could get a chance to avoid being a terminal ed student."

As he was letting me out of his grip, I realized what he was saying. "Aw fuck T.C., I hate that I was so crazy saying what I said."

With a smile on his face that was more like a smirk, T.C. smugly said, "Not really, the time here has allowed me time to take classes to study for my high school equivalency. I have taken and passed the first three out of a five-part test for my GED. If I had not been incarcerated I would be sitting in a classroom looking out the window bored out of my mind." My face was frozen, I could not tell if TC was serious or joking.

He immediately started laughing, looking out the glass door, motioning to Ron that he had pulled off the ruse.

"Touché, that was a good one. You got me." I actually felt good that T.C. was in a joking mood. I did not know what to expect given my last experience with him.

"Before you know it, I'll be out of here and back home, hanging with the boys," T.C. said to further let me know that he was not holding a grudge for what I said.

"Right," I responded, "this shit will be over before you know it".

Unfortunately for T.C. he would have another 4 years in Ravenville. His mother's petition to get him released when he was 16 was blocked by Black, and he was incarcerated for another two years. When he turned 18, the court authorized his release — contingent upon his joining the armed forces.

However, T.C. did — while behind bars — get his high-school diploma.

CHAPTER 3

I moved to Petersville with my family on Easter morning in 1952. My mother and father were just getting back together after being separated for almost two years. We had been living in Chicago with my mother's sister. My siblings and I were all born in Memphis, Tennessee and had been living like nomads since the separation.

Unfortunately, it took the death of my oldest brother Ralph to get my parents back together. A rival neighborhood gang had killed Ralph in Chicago as he was walking home from school. Ralph was not a gang member, but we were living with my aunt (my mother's sister) and our cousins Mark and Sydney were gang members. In 1952, if you lived in a black neighborhood on the west side of Chicago, very few people survived without belonging to a street gang.

My brother Ralph was just a year older than me, but he was my idol. He was 13 but nearly 6 feet tall. Our father was 6 feet 4 inches and had played baseball in high school. Ralph looked, walked and talked so much like my dad. He made good grades and was the man of the house since my parent's separation.

When my parents separated my mother packed us up and moved to Chicago to live with her younger sister. My father had moved to Petersville, Missouri to live with his cousins.

My mother and father met as teenagers in the Mississippi delta in Tallahatchie County. My father's family were farmers in Mississippi who owned land. My great-great grandfather, George Washington Mattox, was a slave who lived on the Mattox plantation. According to my mother, the plantation owner, Leonard Mattox, was my great-great grandfather's father. Like many slave owners, he treated the slave women as his own personal property and took whatever liberties he desired.

When Mattox died he left his son George about 400 acres. He had no family and his slave child George was the only child he had. After years of legal battles from other white property owners who challenged the legality of a will leaving property to children born as slaves, a court ran by reconstruction judges declared the will legal.

My mother got pregnant with my brother Ralph when she was just 15. My father was three years older and they married in 1938. The only work for a black person in 1938 was farming. My parents lived on my mother's family farm. Like a lot of young black men and women living in the south, life under Jim Crow segregation was intolerable. So, with a young 14-month-old baby, my parents left Mississippi moving north to the big city: Memphis. They settled on the south side of Memphis where the majority of black people lived in the early 1940's. I was born in Memphis in 1941.

My mother worked as a waitress for a chain of restaurants that catered to a black clientele. My father was a truck driver. He also liked to gamble and got caught in what they call the sporting life.

Just as my parents started to get settled in Memphis, the Japanese bombed Pearl Harbor. To the surprise of my mother and both sides of their family, my dad joined the US Army two weeks after the bombing. All of his friends were shocked. My dad told me that his friends were telling him he was stupid and crazy signing up to fight for a country that still only saw him as a nigger. My dad, undaunted. ignored them and joined up anyway. He spent his entire time in Europe as a truck driver. He returned home in 1945.

When Ralph got killed my father came to Chicago and literally begged my mother to leave Chicago and move to Petersville.

The neighborhood we moved to in Petersville was called the Southend. It was considered rough and dangerous, but compared to Chicago, Petersville was like Disneyland to us. We moved into the second floor of a two-family flat owned by my father's first cousin Pleas Green, who lived downstairs with his wife Ella.

I met Ron and George on the same day we moved to Petersville. I had just finished eating dinner when my mother called me to come downstairs. When I got there, she was sitting on the couch talking to George and Ron.

"Billy, these are two boys who came by to welcome you to the neighborhood. Isn't that nice of them?" All three of us lowered our heads and looked at the ground. "Introduce yourself to them," she said.

"I'm Billy Strayhorn," I mumbled.

"I'm Ron and this is Snake — I mean George. Snake is just his nickname."

"Why don't y'all go outside and get acquainted?" my mother suggested. We headed out the door and into the streets. There was no front porch, so when you walked out the front door, you walked right onto the sidewalk. Instead of front yards with flowers and grass like our house in Memphis had, there were pieces of broken glass and trash strewn all over the place. Because our flat was so close to Panama Red's, our front always stayed littered with wine, beer and liquor bottles. When we got outside, George immediately started picking up the trash that had accumulated since that morning.

"Why are you doing that?" I asked. "This is the front of *my* house."

"I work for your cousin, Mr. Pleas. I am supposed to pick up the trash twice a day — *every* day," George responded.

"Mr. Pleas said you and your family are from Chicago," Ron said sarcastically.

Hearing the sarcasm in his voice, I said, "I think he told you that we came here from Chicago. We are FROM Memphis."

George drawled sarcastically, "If y'all are FROM Memphis, what were y'all DOING IN Chicago?"

"None of y'all's business," I responded.

Ron and George looked at each other and started laughing.

"Mr. Pleas told us to see if you wanted to walk with us to school tomorrow. You are probably going to be in our room. We are both in the seventh grade," George said.

"That's okay with me, if it's okay with y'all," I said, trying not to show how glad I was. Starting a new school is hard enough. Not knowing anyone is even more traumatic.

"We leave at 7:30 in the morning. That gives us plenty of time to get there and talk on the way," Ron added.

Ron came by the next morning on time. School did not start for an hour and it was only a 15-minute walk from my house. I was ready and waited for him at the bottom of the stairs. It was a cool morning, which meant it was light-jacket weather. After stopping at my house, Ron and I walked up the street to George's house. He lived in the biggest house on the block — and the biggest house I had ever seen.

"George lives with his uncle, Mr. Connors. My daddy says he is the richest and most powerful black man in the Southend," Ron said as we walked through the wrought-iron fence surrounding the front yard of the house. The house looked like a castle.

Ron said, "Your cousin, Mr. Pleas, is the second-richest in the Southend, my daddy says."

"What does his uncle do?" I asked.

"I don't know for sure," he said, "but I heard my daddy say that he has his hands in everything."

"Ronnie?" George yelled as he jumped off the porch. "Did you ask him to join our gang?"

The only knowledge I had of gangs were the ones I saw in Chicago — and I did not want to have anything to do with them. Besides, my mother would kill me if she found out I was in a gang after what had just happened to my brother Ralph.

"Nah, I was waiting until we got to school so he could meet the other members," Ron said.

"I don't want to wait," said George. "Let's ask him now. Hey, boy, you want to join our gang?"

Reluctant to say no outright, I responded, "I ain't your boy, Leroy. What kind of gang is it?"

"It's a gang," George said. "You DO know what a gang is, don't you?"

"Yeah I know what a gang is. There were a bunch of gangs in my neighborhood in Chicago."

The gang that Ron and George were referring to was nothing like the gangs I had seen in Chicago. The gang they were talking about was merely a group of little boys like myself who hung out together.

The gang members — Teddy "T.C." Chambers, Demetrius "Meat" Walker, Wiley Fentress and Leonard "Doc" Marcus — had grown up together and lived within two blocks of each other.

When we got to school, Fentress, Doc, and Meat were on the sidewalk practicing drill-team moves and TC was throwing dice against the wall. Ron introduced me to everybody as Mr. Pleas' cousin from Chicago. Everybody knew my cousin owned Panama Red's, and that gave me status. They all came over and spoke to me — except for T.C. He just kept throwing the dice against the wall until Ron went over and yelled at him.

"Hey, T.C. Come on over and meet the new kid. He just got in from Chicago."

"I heard you. I'm busy and I know he ain't goin' nowhere soon," T.C. mumbled as he continued to throw the dice.

Ron came over and whispered to me, "He's cool. He will be alright by the time the school bell rings."

I stood around for the next 20 minutes, answering a thousand questions about where I was from and what I had seen in Chicago. I immediately felt comfortable with these guys.

We were all in the same seventh- and eighth-grade classroom. Those years went by uneventfully. We graduated from elementary school in 1954, and were all looking forward to going to the same high school — except for T.C. He had been designated "terminally uneducable."

On May 17th of the same year, the U.S. Supreme Court ruled in *Brown vs. Topeka, Kansas, Board of Education* that separate school districts were unconstitutional. The Petersville School Board voted immediately to desegregate its public schools. Initially, that meant our crew would have to attend Madison High School, an all-white high school that was closer to where we lived. But George's mother made a telephone call to a member of the Petersville School Board and arranged to get all of us a permissive transfer. Essentially, it was a waiver that allowed us to attend Booker Washington High School — one of the two high schools for blacks. The permissive transfer policy was instituted to allow white kids who lived in black school-attendance areas to transfer to any school of their choice within the school district. We used it to get out of attending a white school.

Still — even with the permissive transfer — high school broke up our crew somewhat. Ron, George, Wiley, Leonard and I all were assigned a college-prep curriculum. Meat was assigned what was called a general-education format. Wiley's and Leonard's parents, along with a lot of middle-income blacks from the Southend, took advantage of a relaxed housing-discrimination law and moved out of the Southend, but both stayed enrolled at Booker Washington.

I graduated from high school in 1958. The civil-rights movement was in its emerging stage. Dwight D. Eisenhower was president. Rhythm-and-blues — or what the white boys later called rock-and-roll — was just becoming popular. Music by The Drifters, Smokey Robinson and the Miracles, The Platters and The Moonglows was being sung by black teenagers on street corners in every urban city in the U.S.

While 90 percent of all the teenagers I knew were getting into R&B, Ron and I had started listening to jazz. It was our way of trying to look more mature than our peers. Things were changing rapidly in the world around us — and we were absorbing much of it.

CHAPTER 4

Selecting a college to attend was not a difficult process when we graduated from high school.

In 1958, a black high school graduate did not have many choices. The black colleges were still the higher-education choice for most black students who could afford to go. Ron and I decided to go to Hampton Institute in Hampton, Virginia.

It was the college that Booker T. Washington had attended — and it was affordable. My Cousin Pleas paid my first-year tuition, and I got a job to pay for my other expenses. In my junior year, I joined the Reserve Officers Training Corps, which picked up my tuition and gave me a stipend. The hook was I had to spend two years in the U.S. Army after graduation.

I had started dating Ron's cousin Janice Martin when I was a senior in high school. She was two years behind me in school. Our relationship was almost exclusively an "air-mail romance" during my first year of college because my job prevented my coming home for holidays.

During my sophomore year, my parents sent me money so I could come home for Thanksgiving. Wiley, Leonard and George also were home for the holiday. Wiley and Leonard both were attending Morehouse College in Atlanta, Ga. George decided to attend Oberlin College in Oberlin, Ohio. Leonard was in the pre-medical program while Wiley pursued a degree in business. Meat did not go to college. He had become one of the rare black people to attend the Petersville Police Academy. He was now a probationary policeman.

While I was home, I hung out some with the fellas, but I spent most of my time with Janice, now a high-school senior. I was scheduled to return to Hampton on the Sunday after Thanksgiving, so Janice and I planned to go holiday party-hopping on Saturday night. After several parties and a lot of dancing, I took Janice home.

When we got to her door, we both spent another hour engaged in small-talk in a contest to see who would suggest going inside first. Finally, I asked her for a glass of water. I could almost hear a sigh of relief in her voice as she invited me in.

"You don't have to worry about noise," Janice whispered as she closed the door behind me. "My sister is an extremely sound sleeper."

The kitchen in her house was a straight shot down a hallway from the front door. The hallway also served as the family TV room. When Janice got to the kitchen door, I grabbed her arm and pulled her back into the hallway. Before she could resist, I planted a kiss on her lips.

Her passionate response caused me to lose my balance. As I started to fall backward, I felt the edge of the TV-room couch, and I gave in to the momentum. We lay there and kissed for what seemed like hours — but was really five minutes. I took full advantage of the moment's passion and started to run my hands all over Janice's body. I shifted my bodyweight to reverse our positions so I would end up on top of her. The window behind the couch had begun to steam up from our intensity.

I thought about stopping, but since I did not sense or get any resistance from Janice, I stroked her thighs. She was wearing an ankle-length wool skirt and a knit-wool, pull-over sweater. Both of us were virgins, which made the act of penetration clumsy. Recalling what I had heard from "experienced brothers" of the street, I faked it as if I knew what I was doing.

We both spent the next two months worried to death whether she was pregnant. She wasn't. And we decided to postpone having sex again without using protection. Birth-control pills were non-existent for a teenager and abortions were illegal.

During our junior year, Ron and I decided to become lawyers. We also had set our sights on getting admitted to law schools at Harvard or Yale. We applied at the beginning of our senior year at Hampton. We were content with our selections until we had a conversation with our history professor, Walter Jones. Dr. Jones had Ph.D. in history and a law degree. He was one of the more popular instructors on campus. We were in the college cafeteria one day when Dr. Jones came to our table with his tray of food and decided to talk to us about our future.

"Mr. Jackson and Mr. Strayhorn," he bellowed in a deep baritone that sounded as if he had been trained in opera. "What are you two men planning to do with your lives after you graduate?"

We responded in unison: "We're going to law school."

"That sounds good. Have you decided where you want to go?"

"Our first choice is Harvard and our second choice is Yale," Ron said.

"And what is your third choice?"

"We don't have one," I responded. "Yale or Harvard wouldn't dare refuse us."

Eyebrows raised, Mr. Jones said, "I have one question for you: What if neither of the two schools admits you? Do you have any idea the number of Negro lawyers who have been accepted and graduated from Yale or Harvard's law schools?"

We shook our heads, indicating no.

"I don't know, either, but you can bet it is less than the number of fingers I have on both of my hands," Professor Jones said.

"As a safety valve, I think applying to Howard might not be a bad idea," he suggested. "Things were a little better when I graduated from law school in 1940, but not enough. Even after passing the New York state bar exam, I found it hard to make a living. I hung up a shingle and tried to make a living in private practice. Although black people needed a lot of legal help, they did not have any money to pay. I barely made enough money to eat. I took a job teaching, which was *supposed* to be temporary and part-time."

We took his advice and applied to Howard's law school and — just as he predicted — we were not accepted at either Harvard or Yale. Yale did not even send us the customary boilerplate rejection letter. But Howard accepted us.

I still had my military obligation to complete but was able to get a waiver to go to law school.

While we were at Hampton, the whole world changed in front of our eyes. John F. Kennedy was elected president in 1960. Dr. Martin Luther King Jr. had civil rights in full-throttle. Ron and I helped organize — and participated in — freedom rides and sit-ins. We had joined the Hampton chapter of the Student Non-Violent Coordinating Committee (SNCC) and spent the summer of 1960 in rural Georgia and Alabama, helping to register people to vote. In Georgia, we were arrested and spent five days in a county jail. When one of the white deputy sheriffs pushed Ron, he ignored the instructions he had been given about not responding. Ron yelled at the deputy. "You don't have to push me! I can walk!"

"We got us a live, proper-talking nigger from up North," the guard responded. He was holding a stick, which he shoved into Ron's lower back. When Ron turned around, I heard a loud noise that sounded like wood hitting wood. One of the deputies had hit Ron on the back of the head. A third guard pulled his revolver and pointed it at the rest of us. The other deputy continued to hit Ron on his shoulders and back. I felt helpless and sick. That was the last time we participated in any SNCC activities. Ron said he could never be non-violent again. We decided the best thing for us to do was to graduate from college, become lawyers, go home and try to help change things there.

Going to law school at Howard proved to be the best decision we could have made. And something that Professor Jones said stuck with me: "Even if you are accepted at Harvard or Yale, white America would not look at you any differently than a Howard law school graduate. You would still be seen as a black lawyer."

After we graduated from Howard's law school in 1966, Ron went back to Petersville to study for the bar exam. I still had a two-year commitment to Uncle Sam. The army offered me an assignment to the Judge Advocate General Corps, an automatic promotion to captain — and the stipulation that I serve four years. I declined and was assigned to the basic-training course for officers at Fort Leonard Wood in rural Missouri. The fort was nicknamed "Little Korea" because of the weather and the rigors of its basic-training program.

I reported at Ft. Leonard Wood on June 6, 1966. After 8 weeks of basic training I was assigned to attend the adjutant school at Fort Benjamin Harrison, Indiana. An adjutant was the equivalent of a personnel director in civilian life. Afterward, I was assigned to the 545th Personnel Service Company at Fort Holibrid, Maryland. The 545th was a support unit for a number of small transportation units being dispatched to South Vietnam.

So, within six months after graduating from law school, I found myself in Vietnam. I arrived in Vietnam on a chartered commercial plane on January 10, 1967. We landed at Ton Son Nhut Base. The air base was located near Saigon. Ton Son Nhut was the focal point of the initial United States deployment and buildup in South Vietnam in the 1960's.

While looking through the window of the plane as it was landing, I could see ground fire from tracer rounds being fired from a distance as the pilot was announcing welcome to Vietnam. My orders said I was supposed to report to the 90th replacement battalion, but arriving at night meant I would have to sleep on a cot at the air base. Transporting troops at night was only done in the case of an emergency because of the danger of an ambush.

The average age of a soldier sent to Vietnam was 19 which made me a father figure to a lot of the men who were on my plane. What they did not know was that I was scared shitless. After we deplaned, we were shuttled to a waiting room inside the terminal. We were given a blanket and pillow and ushered back outside and told to go inside a large tent. Inside the tent, there were cots where we would sleep for the night.

As we settled in we could hear light weapons and see tracers racing across the sky from a distance. The NCO directing us told us not to worry about the gun fire you see or hear, it's the gun fire you don't hear that is the problem. In other words when you get shot you hear nothing.

After about an hour we all settled down to attempt sleeping. I don't think any of us really got any sleep. The gun fire lasted all night. We were awakened at 6am the next morning. After eating a pretty decent breakfast, we were told to go to the waiting room where we were last night. Our duffel bags were lined up against the wall and we were told to get our bags and board a green camouflaged bus. I was told that, because I was an officer, I could ride in the escort jeep, but I decided to ride the bus with the enlisted men.

As was the case in the army, no one ever told you where you were going, but my guess was we were all going to the 90th Replacement Battalion.

After about an hour ride on a highway where the scenery was dotted with rice paddies and tropical jungle foliage, we arrived at this huge complex of Quonset huts and tents with hundreds of soldiers.

The bus dropped me off first at the officers' quarters, a Quonset hut set up as a barracks that had a shower inside. The enlisted men were taken to the tent barracks.

I unpacked and took a shower. One of the officers sharing the barracks with me gave me the rundown on the process. He said the normal amount of time spent at the replacement battalion was two days unless your orders are changed. He looked at my orders and told me that transport to my unit came every day at 9am. I was assigned to the 4th Transportation Battalion, which was part of the 1st Logistical Command located in Saigon. The 4th Transportation Battalion was a stevedore company organized to load and unload military supply ships in the Saigon Harbor.

Armed with that information, I decided to cool out. It was 10:30, an hour and half before lunch so I decided to take a nap to catch up on the sleep I lost last night.

I was so tired that I don't remember falling asleep. I was awakened by one of the other officers at 11:45 for lunch. The officers and enlisted men ate lunch in the same place, a large tent in the middle of the camp. While walking up to the camp I heard a voice yell out. "Hey runt, what the hell are you doing here?!"

That voice was recognizable to me anywhere. I turned and standing in the enlisted mess line was T.C. I rushed over to him and we both hugged each other in total surprise.

"I thought you went to law school?" T.C. inquired. "Did you volunteer?"

"I had an ROTC scholarship which required me to serve two years of military service. The only good thing is that I get to serve as an officer. But look at you, those stripes make you an E7, a sergeant first-class and is that a special forces patch? You are a bad ass."

T.C. just smiled and did not respond to my observation. "It looks like you are just arriving in. I am completing my third tour of duty in this shit hole. My buddies and I are DEROSing (date of estimated return from overseas); we are on our way home," T.C. said.

"Yes, I got in last night. Arrived here at about 9am this morning," I replied.

After going through the lunch line, T.C. and I spent the next two hours updating each other on what we had been doing for the last decade. The T.C. I was talking to was vastly different from the guy I saw blow Baby Ray off that car in 1955. He was a seasoned, mature gladiator. I was sitting next to a man trained to fight wars in the shadows, under the cloak of darkness. In many ways, the court's attempt to rehabilitate T.C. may have made him more dangerous.

T.C. had to leave at three, with his plane departing from Ton Son Nhut at 5. He told me his current enlistment was up and he was going back to Petersville, but did not plan to live there. I told him good luck and to look in on my Mom and Dad when he got back.

36

The next morning, as expected, the transport for the 1st Log Command arrived at 8:30. The bus left at 9, and we arrived at the Command headquarters located in seaport section of Saigon. I spent a year and two months in the "Nam." The usual tour of duty was 13 months, but I extended my tour for a month so I could leave the army upon my return stateside. I took advantage of an army policy that allowed a soldier to be released immediately from active duty if he had fewer than 90 days before his estimated-term expired date. I left Vietnam on March 10, 1968.

The first thing I did when I got back to the States was call home. I talked first with my mother, and then I called Janice and Ron. While stationed in Vietnam, I had taken advantage of not having to pay sales or excise taxes, and I bought a Volkswagen Beetle. It was delivered to the Port of Oakland, and I planned to drive it home. When I told Ron about my plans, he insisted on flying out to California and driving back with me. I accepted his offer without hesitation.

CHAPTER 5

Ron and I hooked up in San Francisco on March 14. It took a full two days for me to get discharged from the Army. It took another day to get my car and Ron and I decided to take in some of the nightlife in San Francisco before getting on the road. We had dinner and went bar hopping to hear some jazz in the Fillmore section of Sam Francisco.

After a couple of nights of partying, Ron and I got on the road for the 32-hour drive to Petersville. Ron made it clear our friendship was not the only reason he volunteered to help me drive home. He spent the first part of the trip drilling me about Vietnam and the army. He used the second part of the trip to sell me on the idea of us starting a law firm and getting involved in politics.

"I came to get you for two reasons," he said. "First, to ask you to help me open a law firm — something we had talked about in law school. Second, I want you to help me get George elected as Democratic committeeman of the Ninth Ward."

"I'll have to pass the bar first," I said. "That's my response to number one. In terms of number two, is George suffering from some type of Oedipus complex about his Uncle?"

"Mr. Connors died two months ago, and George's mother appointed him to replace Connors."

"I'm sorry to hear about old man Connors," I said. "He was always friendly and helpful to me."

"The older heads in the ward resent Rita for appointing him," George explained. "A lot of them think she should appoint one of his cronies. Subsequently, they rebelled and started a rump ward organization and got Harvey Bumstead to run against George."

"I still don't see the problem," I said. "You and I both know how hard it is to beat the ward organization."

"Under normal circumstances your analysis would be correct."

"But what?" I interrupted.

"Bumstead has aligned himself with the Syrians, and they are backing him financially," Ron said.

"I thought the Syrians and Mr. Connors were political allies," I said.

"They were, but George and Mrs. Martin want to be independent. Plus, Rita told them she was going to vote on the Democratic Central Committee the way she wanted. On top of that, the chairman of the central committee died. Rita and George ended up being the swing votes, and they voted against the candidate the Syrians wanted. Rita and George wanted more — and better-paying — patronage jobs. The Syrians told them they would think about it. The other side cut them a deal and gave them what they wanted."

"I can tell the rest of this story myself," I ventured. "They are going after George and Rita!"

"Billy, this is the opportunity for us to leap-frog our dream of securing and using power. Connors' death is like a gift for us. If

George can hold onto the committeeman's seat, we can start to implement the things we've dreamed about since we were in high school," Ron hammered on.

"You mean the dream *you* have had. You always assumed I was in agreement with your grandiose plans to run Petersville."

"The ride won't be the same without you," he said. "Most people can't begin to grasp what I'm talking about."

"If it's that complicated, maybe you should leave it alone," I said sarcastically.

The rest of the drive home, Ron continued to hammer away at how George's election was a unique opportunity for us.

I was unaware Ron had called home and arranged for Janice to put together a homecoming party for Wiley and me. Wiley already knew about it because he had been home for a week. This was the first time he had been home for more than two days since 1963, when he attended his mother's funeral.

When we were close to Petersville, we stopped at a service station for gas. Ron used the opportunity to call Janice to let her know exactly when we would arrive. Once we entered the Petersville city limits, Ron suggested we stop off at Panama Red's for a drink. It sounded like a good idea, and I could surprise my mother.

When we drove up to the house, I thought we had lucked out because there was a parking space right in front. I could not know the space had been reserved for me. As we walked through the door I figured it out — but it was too late. I couldn't believe the number of people there. It looked like a high school reunion. My parents and siblings were the first to greet me. I had been home only once in the last two years, but seeing them that night made me realize how much I had missed my family.

After a few minutes of glad-handing and telling everyone how I was doing, a band started playing the first chords to the Temptations song "Since I Lost My Baby." The music was followed by a voice singing the lyrics. Only two, possibly three, people knew how much I loved the music of the Temptations — especially that song. As I turned to see who was singing the song, someone tapped me on my shoulder.

"Can you still do the Three Step?" a female voice asked.

"That depends," I said, looking in the direction of the voice. When I recognized who it was, I immediately answered yes.

Janice had grown up and was a strikingly-beautiful woman. She had on a black, low-cut, after-five dress with the back out, which exposed her smooth, coal-black skin.

"I almost didn't know who you were," I said, staring her down.

"I'll have to do something about that when I get over being angry with you."

"Angry at me? What did I do — and how can I make it up?"

"You let my cousin come and get you without asking me if I wanted to come. But I think five dinners and at least six movie dates can get you redemption," she laughed, revealing her beautifully-curved lips.

"Can I start tonight?"

"Are you sure you can break away from your friends?"

"It's 7 o'clock now. How long do you think this party is going to last?"

"I told the band to play until 8:30," she said. "After that, a lot of people want to hang out. Friday night is brothers' night out on the Southend. I suspect you will be hanging, too."

"Only if you'll hang out with us."

Before she could answer, I felt a tug on my shirt. My sister Rhonda was pulling me away.

"I'm sorry, Janice, but you cannot hog him," Rhonda said as she pulled me across the room to a table of her friends.

"I will be back!" I yelled. Janice nodded her head in agreement.

"I told you girls he was cute — and he's smart, too," Rhonda said, introducing me to a table of her girlfriends. "And he's a lawyer!"

I spent the rest of the evening at the Panama talking about Vietnam and what I was going to do. Later that evening, Ron and George got a group of us together, including Janice, to go out and bar-hop. Ron and I did not last too long. The fatigue of driving 32 hours began to set in. George ended up taking us home at 10 that evening.

I slept until late in the afternoon the next day and did not wake up until my mother came home from work. She was managing both the restaurant and the tavern now for cousin Pleas. He had been ill and had to slow down. My mother and I had not really talked since I left for college. I seldom wrote home. In fact, my mother had to contact the Red Cross to track me down in Vietnam once because I had not written a letter in four months. When she got home from work, she came into my room to wake me up.

"Are you hungry? I'm cooking pinto beans, ham-hocks and cornbread for dinner," I heard her say as I looked up. She smiled, knowing pinto beans and ham-hocks were my favorite meal.

"I'll wait for the beans," I said.

"It won't be long. I put 'em in water to soak before I left, so they shouldn't take too long to cook. It'll be about an hour."

"Good, that'll give me another half-hour to sleep. Would you wake me up about half-an-hour before you finish?"

"You take your time. I miss you a lot. Billy. I'm so happy to see you."

"I miss you, too, Modear," I said, using a nickname I'd given her years ago. My eyes were swollen from hearing her voice.

Fifteen minutes later, the phone rang. My mother knocked on the door and yelled, "It's Janice." I jumped up and ran to get the phone. My mother handed me the phone and smiled.

"I thought you wanted to sleep."

"Hi, Janice," I said, smiling back at my mother. "I forgot to thank you for helping last night. I had a wonderful time." My mother was listening to every word I said, so I stretched the phone cord back into my room for some privacy.

"What are doing right now?" I asked.

"Nothing. I just got home from the grocery store."

"Why don't you come over to my mom's house and have dinner with us? We're having pinto beans and ham hocks."

"What time do you want me there?"

"Momma said the beans should be finished by 4:30."

"I'll be there."

"One date down and five to go!"

Janice laughed as she hung up the phone. I was wide-awake now. There was something about Janice's voice that excited me. I took a shower, put on some clothes and went into the kitchen.

"I invited Janice over. I hope that is okay," I told my mother.

"There'll be plenty. Janice is a real pretty girl. She's got an education and she has a good job," Modear said.

"I didn't know you ran a dating service."

"I don't, but I can express my opinion. You could do much worse."

Realizing I had no chance of winning in this conversation, I decided not to respond.

Janice came over that afternoon, and we ate and talked with my mother for about an hour. Modear had to be back at The Panama at 6 pm. She now was managing the restaurant for Pleas. I couldn't take my eyes off Janice. She had blossomed over the last 18 months.

After dinner, we decided to go to the movies. She quizzed me all the way to the theater and back about Vietnam. She would have talked through the movie if I hadn't stopped her. Afterward, I drove her home. She was still living with her parents in the Southend. When we got to her house, she invited me in to say hello to her parents.

Although her father had become a bishop in the African Methodist Episcopal Church, he was still serving as pastor at St. Mark's until AME church officials could appoint someone to replace him. Her parents greeted me warmly and then went upstairs.

"I'm going to have a cup of tea," she said. "Would you like one?"

She started walking towards the rear of the house to the kitchen. I followed her and, as we got inside the kitchen door, she grabbed me, pushed me against the refrigerator and kissed me.

"I have wanted to do that since you first walked through the door last night," she said. "I missed you, Billy Strayhorn!"

"*Why* did you miss me?" I asked, pulling her close for a second kiss.

We continued until Janice stopped to ask, "What are your plans for the future, Billy Strayhorn?"

"What future are you talking about? The next few months or the next few years?"

"Both," she said. "I want to know how much of me I need to invest in you."

At that moment, the teapot began whistling. "Do you like red-zinger tea?" I asked. "It's what the hippies drink."

"My intentions, Mr. Strayhorn, are to convince you to marry me. I know I am being a bit forward. I want to make sure you understand how I feel about you. I have loved you since the first time I saw you. You're the smartest and handsomest man I know."

Once the tea bags brewed, Janice handed me a cup. I drank it slowly, trying to absorb what she has just said.

"Take your time," she said. "I don't need a response right now. We need to spend some time getting to know each other again."

"Whew, I'm glad you said that."

"Drink up. I got an early day ahead of me. I teach a Sunday School class I haven't prepared for. I'll talk to you tomorrow," she said, putting her cup down on the counter. She grabbed my arm and kissed me again. "I want to make sure you'll be back." Then Janice walked me to the door and said goodnight.

My mother was asleep when I got home, and my father was out — as usual. My other siblings and I had always thought that our old man had another woman, but we couldn't prove it. I think my mother knew, but she had long since decided to make her marriage work, no matter what. When I returned, I saw a message from Ron that my mother had left on the refrigerator. He and George were at a bar called The Living Room and would wait there for me until 10 that evening. It was only 9 p.m. so I went to meet them.

Calling this place "The Living Room" was an oxymoron if there ever was one. The place gave the name "Hole-In-The-Wall" some class. The floors were wooden, and the doors were the old revolving kind, reminiscent of the ones in old western TV shows. However, it did have a nice crowd for a Tuesday night.

When I arrived, I had to park on a side-street next to the alley. This was one of those times I wished I were driving something less ostentatious. As I got out of my car, suddenly the flashing lights of a police car hit me. A familiar voice yelled.

"Are you crazy, parking that car on this street? You surely have been away from the 'hood too long."

I immediately recognized the voice and barked back, "That's why they have police, right? To protect and serve? I should be able to park anywhere!"

"What's up, Billy? It's good to see you again, Brother! Glad to see that you survived the Nam."

"Who let you join the police force?" I laughed. Right after high school, Meat got on the force the same way everyone did in 1967: With the help of a sponsor. Meat's sponsor was Black.

That night, Meat was riding with a white policeman, who was immediately impressed with the fact that I had been in the war in Southeast Asia.

"You were in Vietnam?" his partner asked. "It is a pleasure to meet you, sir." As I shook his hand, Meat put his arm around my shoulder and whispered, "I have him trained well." We both laughed. I wanted to tell the white boy that, in hindsight, I should not have gone to the Nam, I was against the war; I saw it was a waste of young lives in a senseless war. At the time, I thought my going added credibility to the war. If I had protested, maybe I

46

could have saved someone's life. But I kept it to myself because I knew this patriotic redneck would not understand.

Meat and I talked briefly. He told me no one would bother my car. This was his patrol area, and he would make sure nobody touched it. I told him I was meeting Ron and Snake inside.

"Have fun," Meat said, waving as he and his partner got back into the police car. "I'll see you later."

Ron and George were sitting at the bar when I came in. Ron waved for me to come over. As I sat down, Ron had the bartender bring out a bottle of Moet White Star Champagne that had been chilling behind the bar.

"I didn't think you were coming after your mother told me who you were with," Ron said as he poured some champagne into the glass. "My cousin is on a mission, Brother — and you are it."

"A cynic would say you put her up to trying to seduce me," I said, winking at George.

"I'm just glad to have you back, Brother," George said, raising his glass in a toast.

"It's good to be back, Mr. Connors, Jr.," I responded. George and Ron both laughed and proposed another toast.

"I hope Ron and I can convince you to serve as manager for my campaign," George said. "I need people running my shit who I can trust. The Syrians have co-opted most of the workers. The only ones who've stayed with me are the older ones who were with my uncle from the beginning. There are almost 200 city, state or federal patronage workers who belong to the Ninth Ward. More than half have stopped paying dues. Several of the Democratic officeholders have pledged their support to Bumstead."

I interrupted George with a loud sarcastic laugh. "Let me see if I understand what you are telling me. Your uncle, who ran the Ninth Ward like a little fiefdom, died. This is the same uncle who most politicians — both black and white — either respected or feared. What did you think the whites and the blacks who feared and envied him were going to do? You need to soak your face in rock-salt and toughen up. You sound too naïve for the politics of Petersville. Your uncle didn't leave a will giving you the committeeman's seat and all its spoils."

"I don't expect that it will be easy," George responded defensively.

"Then stop your complaining. Your hand is still better than Bumstead's."

"That's why we need you here to help us, Billy," George quickly shot back. "We need a clear thinker."

"Ron knows more about what is going on than I do."

"We got a plan; we just need your help to pull it off," Ron chimed in.

"That's where I am confused," I said. "You and Ron are much more schooled in the political process than I am."

"You're not going to get away with that kind of bullshit excuse," Ron said as he motioned to the bartender to let him know we were moving. "You are a natural. Look at how you just analyzed the Bumstead situation. Let's move over there to that booth to talk. Once I explain the plan, it will be clear to you how you fit in."

Once we were seated, I said, "Okay, I just want to know how you plan to do this and where I fit in. And can I get an answer that doesn't require a lengthy soliloquy from you?"

"Do you remember how we won the class and student-body presidential elections in high school?" Ron asked.

48

"Yeah, I remember what you did. You had George file as a stalking-horse candidate. He stayed in the race until the nominations closed and then withdrew."

"Masterful, wasn't it?" George beamed as he and Ron gave each other five.

"I've devised another version of it that is going to fuck everybody up. I found a man with the same last name as Bumstead. He's 75 years old. He is going to file at 4:59 p.m. on the day the filing for the August primary closes," Ron said, "and then he'll go on an extended vacation to visit his family in Gulf Port, Mississippi."

"You don't think George can win straight-up against Bumstead?" I asked.

"I want to *guarantee* George wins!" Ron said. "I don't think we'll have this opportunity again — and I don't want to blow it!"

"I wish you and George all the success in the world, but I'm still not sure I want to live in Petersville," I said. "I've known you and George for a long time and I know this is something you're really committed to, but going to Vietnam made me want to stop and smell the roses. I've been on a roller coaster since I graduated from law school. I was thinking about going back out to California and visiting Carlos. He told me to look him up when I got out of the service."

"I hear what you're saying, Billy, I really do, but you, me — none of us have a choice. Our fate is predestined. Somebody has to step up and lead our community. I'll be damned if I let it fall to the Bumsteads of the world by default."

"It's early yet. You said you'd be here until April, so we still got some time to get you on board."

"There's also another reason I need you to stay. You know I've been working in the public defender's office for almost 18 months. Since I started working for George, the Syrians have been putting a lot pressure on my boss to fire me. That's why I want us to go into private practice together. You know this is something we have always talked about."

I stared at Ron, unable to give him an answer to any of his requests. He had all these plans for me, and I had barely been home a few days. I needed time to figure out what I wanted to do with my life — on my own terms.

CHAPTER 6

I spent the next three weeks hanging out with Janice and my family.

In early April, I called Ron and asked him to go to lunch with me. He agreed and told me to meet him at the Metropolitan Café, a soul-food restaurant popular at lunchtime with black lawyers and black politicians. After passing the bar two years ago, Ron joined the public defender's office and quickly became a legend. He won acquittals on his first six cases, setting a record for the Petersville Public Defender's office. I found out about it that day at lunch. As we were coming through the door, someone yelled, "Six Shooter!" Ron waved and kept walking.

"What does "Six Shooter" mean?" I asked

"It's a nickname given to me by the news media when I won a record six cases in a row," Ron answered.

"That *is* impressive! What was the previous record?"

"Three."

"Damn, Bro, that means you doubled the record," I said. "And your boss is giving you static? That's fucked-up."

We were halfway through lunch when one of the waitresses began screaming.

"Oh, Lord, oh, Lord! Martin Luther King has been shot! The radio just said Dr. King has been shot!" she kept screaming.

There was absolute silence in the restaurant. I got up from my chair and walked back to the kitchen area to listen to a radio playing near the dishwasher. The announcer said that Martin Luther King Jr. had been shot in the head on the balcony of a motel in Memphis, Tennessee. I still could not believe what I heard.

Ron and several other customers had walked back to listen by now. Ron and I just looked at each other. Like most people, we were in a state of shock. I grabbed Ron by the arm and took him out to the car. The street was blocked with people who had heard on their car radios what had happened and has just stopped their cars in the middle of the street. Traffic was jammed for three or four blocks. A police car had stopped and a white police officer was talking to people, trying to get them to move. Ron walked over and told him what had happened.

"I don't give a fuck!" he yelled at Ron. "If these people don't stop blocking my street, I'm going to start arresting them."

"I don't think that would be a good idea," I offered.

"And who the fuck are you?" he yelled. "I don't give a fuck what you think! You better tell these people to move their cars or I'll start writing tickets!"

The restaurant was at the corner of Pierce and Washington Avenue, one of the busiest intersections in the Southend. In addition to the Metropolitan Café, there was a black-owned savings-and-loan company, a black-owned beautician and barber school and a private, black social club owned and operated by a group called the South End Waiters Club. The policeman ignored our warning and started writing tickets.

There was a small, hole-in-the-wall bar right off the corner called the Talk of the Town that was owned by Jackson Green, a small-time front-man for the Syrian crime bosses. His place was patronized by a lot of brothers who had done time and were not afraid of the police. When a few of them came outside and saw the police officer writing tickets, they went smooth-off.

They started cursing and telling him to back off. He ignored them and kept on writing. I was still trying to talk to him, but it was useless. Sensing something ugly was about to happen, I went inside the Metropolitan and called the police district where Meat worked. They said he was off-duty, so I called the Fourth District Police station.

The district commander, James Rangle, was the first black in the Petersville Police Department to hold that position. I explained to him what was going on, and he said he would dispatch some black officers to the scene. I asked him to see if he could contact Meat and send him over, since he had grown up in the neighborhood. Rangle agreed. I hung up the phone and went back outside, where things were beginning to escalate.

Several people were starting to form human shields around the cars. The white cop's arrogance and racism made him act ambivalent to the anger and frustration the crowd was feeling. He grabbed the handle of his revolver and told the crowd to move. The next thing I saw was a brick flying out of the crowd and slamming upside the officer's head. Blood shot everywhere as the impact of the brick hitting his head knocked him to the ground. Luckily for the cop, another police car pulled up. Meat and another black policeman ran over to the wounded cop. Meat began to plead for calm as the other policeman moved the white officer to a safer area. Recognizing Meat, the crowd backed off a little. I grabbed Meat's arm and pulled him aside.

"The cracker provoked the shit, Meat," I whispered in his ear. "He started writing tickets immediately after the announcement that King was shot."

"These people here are going to be even more pissed off now," Meat said. "I just heard over the two-way radio that King died. All vacation and leaves have been cancelled. Riots have broken out in Washington, D.C., Chicago, Detroit, Philly, Los Angeles and almost every big city.

"They're expecting things to blow up here, too. I'd advise you to get off the street as soon as you can. The mayor is coming on TV at 5 o'clock with a special appeal for calm. Welcome home, Brother."

"Billy, let's go!" Ron yelled. The traffic had begun to let up. We got in the car and drove off. I dropped Ron off at the public defender's office and went home.

My mother was sitting in the living room, crying in front of the TV. Pleas had closed Panama Red's and sent everyone home. Even my old man came home early. He normally did not have a lot to say about things, but this was an exception. He and my mother were sitting in front of the TV watching the news.

"Talking about the Vietnam War was his downfall," my old man kept saying. "He wouldn't stay in his place — and white people were not going to allow that!"

My mother didn't say anything. I hugged her and went into my room. As I closed the door, tears began to flow down my face uncontrollably. I started having flashbacks of Ron and me on the grass at the Washington Monument during the March on Washington in 1963. When Dr. King spoke, you had to listen. I never cared much for his non-violent approach, but I admired his courage and diligence. I felt the same way about his death as I did when my older brother Ralph died.

The reaction in Petersville was mild compared to what happened in Chicago, Detroit or Washington, D.C. Some downtown store windows were broken and looted. This lasted one night. The Petersville mayor organized a bi-racial, interfaith council that conducted a memorial service and a huge march that co-opted the black community. The mayor also talked the executive committee of the city's chamber of commerce into establishing a dialogue group that would meet once a month to discuss the race problem in the city.

The mastermind behind what became a successful strategy was Popich and Associates, a public-relations firm that worked for the Petersville Chamber of Commerce. Hank Popich, the chief executive officer of the firm, had spent a large chunk of his life in the Southend. His father was one the grocers who plotted to keep Ron's father from expanding into the grocery business. When he was young, his family lived above the store. Hank and Ron were friends and used to spend the night at each other's house.

Ron's father had wanted to expand his store into a full-service grocery store. Popich's dad owned a grocery store in the Southend. Ron's old man and Popich's dad had been friends until Mr. Jackson decided to expand. Although Ron's father had the financial capacity to do so, the white and Jewish grocers conspired with the wholesalers to prevent him from buying from them. Ron told me about the time his father went to a wholesale produce market to try and arrange lines of credits to purchase produce. Every wholesaler refused to extend him credit. Initially, they told him he would need letters of credit from a bank. After he secured such letters, they told him he would need to agree to purchase a certain amount of produce each week to make it worth their while. They continued to come up with a different requirement every time until one day one of the owners pulled him aside and told him it was futile to keep coming down to the market — they simply were not going to do business with him.

55

The owner said the other grocers had told the farmers if anyone did business with him, they would lose their business.

Mr. Jackson also believed that George's uncle, Jim Connors, had something to do with his not being able to expand. Mr. Jackson had never been a supporter of Connors. He was an "Abraham Lincoln Republican." He also suspected Connors had something to do with the run-around he got from the city inspectors when he tried to get his architectural plans for the expansion approved. They lost his application forms twice, and they demanded of him things no one else had to do. This caused some tension between George and Ron, but they agreed not to talk about it in order to preserve their friendship.

Popich's uncle had been the councilman for the Ninth Ward for more than 20 years, until Jim Connors ran a candidate that unseated him in 1954. Popich had parlayed his familiarity with blacks into a business opportunity. He touted himself as an expert on how to deal with the black community. Through the black newspapers, black ministers and black politicians, he was able to control what went on in the black community. If the chamber of commerce needed a tax proposal or school bond-issue passed, Popich was the bagman who paid off the ministers and politicians. He would purchase ads in the black newspapers to get their support, and he would get the support of the civic organizations like the Urban League and the NAACP through direct contributions.

After returning home, I had dozed off for about an hour when my mother came into the room and said Ron was on the telephone.

"Did you see that punk Popich on the TV?" Ron asked.

"Yes, I saw him."

"White folks are a motherfucker! They go out and get a Jew to counsel them on how black folks should mourn. They organize a group of pork-chop nigger preachers and jelly-backed nigger leaders to tell *us* to keep the lid on! Mark my word, Billy, Petersville is going to be the only city in this country that does not riot."

"Whoa, Ron, I know you're not suggesting that we need to riot."

"We need to do something unpredictable," he said. "White folks have been used to a milky-toast response from us."

"Fuck all of that emotional, cathartic bullshit," I said. "We have a plan, right? Let's make it work. It would be a total waste of time reacting to Popich's shit. Popich is able to do what he does because he has a plan that he works on 24 hours a day, every day. Our commitment has to be the same."

Ron was silent for a minute. For the first time, he had to respect his own shit coming right back at him. I did not wait for him to respond. "What's up with the election?"

"You, George and I need to meet for an update and strategy session," Ron said. "George and I usually meet every Saturday morning at Hattie's for breakfast. Can you meet us there this Saturday?"

The time sounded bad for me, but I agreed.

Ron called me at 6 a.m. Saturday. "Get up, Brother. I'm on my way to pick you up."

"Fuck, Ron! It's too early to do anything," I moaned.

"Just get up. I'm on my way."

I got up and stumbled into the bathroom. After washing up and slipping on some clothes, I went into the kitchen and got a cup of coffee. Modear made a pot of coffee every morning, regardless of who was up.

The horn of Ron's car was so loud, it woke the entire block. I ran down and got in his car. A light snow was falling, just enough to cover the streets. Only in Petersville would it snow in April. I had not seen snow for almost three years. Ron drove a 1966 Kelly green Mustang convertible — and he drove like a bat out of hell. The streets were slippery, but that didn't faze him. I was scared out of my wits by Ron's reckless driving in the snow. When we finally got to Hattie's, I jumped out of the car.

"Remind me never to let you drive me anywhere. Do you have a driver's license?

"Yes, I do," Ron said, smiling as he got out of the car.

"I can't tell."

"There's George. Let's get something to eat and talk about my driving later."

George had secured a table in a small, private room in Hattie's. We all sat down and ordered a Southern breakfast of grits, smothered chicken, pork sausage, eggs, biscuits and strawberry jam. George started the meeting by giving an update of the campaign.

"I have very little to report," he said. "We had a meeting scheduled for Thursday, but the assassination of Dr. King forced us to cancel it."

"What about our stalking horse? Is he still a go?" I asked.

"I talked to him Monday," Ron said. "He's ready. He wants — and needs — the money."

"How many of Connors' workers can you count on to work with you?" I asked.

"About half of them still come to the meetings and pay their dues. The campaign hasn't started, so it's hard to say who will stay."

58

"What is the dues structure?"

"One percent of their annual salary."

"One way we could perhaps pull some of the workers who are with Bumstead is to promise to get rid of the dues structure," I suggested. "My old man used to complain all the time that he hated the 1 percent tax your uncle put on them. You could make it a one-time initiation fee when they got their job."

"But where are we going to get money to run the organization?"

"Have fundraisers," I said. "Give them a choice: Sell tickets to the fundraisers or pay dues. That way, those who don't want to sell tickets can continue to pay dues."

"Billy is right, George," Ron chimed in. "We've got to be different! Most of the workers don't care about this political shit. They want to save their jobs so they can continue to feed their families. This 1 percent tax system is just a step above slavery. We could call ourselves the Progressive Ninth Ward Democratic Club."

"That all sounds good, but what does it have to do with kicking Bumstead's ass?" George responded. He got up to get a cup of coffee. It was obvious he wasn't buying the new idea.

"Other than the people in the ward organization and a few others, how many people in the Ninth Ward knows either of you?" I asked.

"They don't know me, but they do know my mother," George said. "She will be the one to pull the votes out for us."

"Don't take this the wrong way, but you both know your uncle ran the ward as a dictatorship," Ron said. "Are you sure your mother can garner the same level of support that your uncle did?"

"It's not my mother — it will be about me," George shot back.

"That's why I asked. I want you to start thinking that way."

George got up and walked back over to the coffeepot. He started to pour a cup of coffee and then stopped. He looked back at Ron. "You are always trying to tell me about how you want me to think. I don't see any difference between you and the Syrians."

I looked at Ron for a reaction, but he just shrugged off George's comment.

"I'm sorry, George. I know I can be pushy," Ron said. "I just want us to win."

"I almost forgot," George said suddenly. "The state presidential caucuses are in two weeks. We will be selecting candidates to the State Democratic Convention in June. The Democratic committee people are responsible for finding a location for the meeting and conducting it. The State Democratic Party has established a set of rules that have to be adhered to."

George took a small booklet out of his coat pocket and handed it to me. "I need you to be our parliamentarian, Billy."

We had been sitting for almost an hour, and George had not brought up the caucus issue. Something was wrong. But when I looked at Ron for a response, I could see he didn't want to talk about it in front of George.

After handing me the caucus rule booklet, George looked at his watch and got up to get his coat.

"I have to leave," he said. "I've got a 9am meeting with some white boys who are trying to put together an endorsement package for the governor's election. It could solve all of our money problems."

"Billy and I will go through the rules booklet and get a report to you by Monday," Ron said. Clearly, he wanted George to feel we were still on the team. And he could see the frustration in my face.

George put on his coat and walked out the door. I waited for George to leave before saying anything to Ron. I got up and sat in George's chair to be closer to Ron.

I leaned over and whispered in his ear. "Are you fucking serious? George is a joke. Is he on something? He is truly a strange-acting motherfucker."

"I agree he's different, but we have to be patient," Ron said. "He still is the best horse we've got to ride — right now."

"Who are you trying to convince of that shit? Me or yourself?" I demanded. "You know goddam well what I am talking about. He isn't focused and he *doesn't* trust you. I don't think he has a clue. I'm almost tempted to say that the brother is on something. Did you see how much sugar he put in his cup of coffee. That is a junkie sign."

"He'll be okay," Ron said calmly. "We'll just have to stay real close to him between now and Election Day."

"You are suffering from a bad case of misplaced optimism if you believe George is up to the task of helping to jumpstart our plan," I said. "But for now, I suggest you stay on top of George."

"I agree. Let's get started on this caucus thing," Ron said.

We both got up, got our coats and left. I was still worried about George, but there was very little I could do but wait and hope for the best. George was the committeeman, and there was very little we could do about it.

CHAPTER 7

George's mother, Rita, was the senior elected party official of the Ninth Ward, a strong Democratic voting ward. Because of the large number of professionals and middle-class black families who lived there, it was known as the silk-stocking ward of the Southend. In 1968, there were 15,000 registered voters in the Ninth Ward. In the previous presidential election, more than 70 percent of the Ninth Ward's registered voters had gone to the polls — and 90 percent of them voted Democratic.

State Democratic Party delegates were allocated on the basis of the percentage of registered voters who cast their ballots for Democrats in the previous presidential election. The Ninth Ward was allotted the largest number of state Democratic delegates in the city.

After reading the rules book, I called George to set up a meeting with him, his mother and Ron to discuss the rules and to plan a strategy to ensure that on Caucus Night, we controlled the delegate selection.

I started by explaining how the meetings were structured. Connors had run the meetings in the past. Mrs. Martin, like most of the committeewomen of her time, had very little to do with ward business. But with the death of Connors, Rita now was the senior Democratic Party official in the Ninth Ward.

After I explained the legal requirements that had to be obeyed by Rita and George, we started talking about the political ramifications.

"The caucus is going to be an important test for us," I said.

"Why do you say that?" George asked. He looked more focused than he had at breakfast the previous Saturday morning.

"Bumstead and his supporters will be trying to embarrass you by stacking the room with his supporters. As I explained before, it's a numbers game."

"The caucus is less than two weeks away," Rita said. "Is that enough time to organize enough people to beat Bumstead?"

"I asked Ron to come up with some plans to make sure we'll win," I said, smiling as I sat down. "That's his specialty."

George also was smiling and nodding in agreement. His mother Rita had a puzzled, what-the-hell-are-you-talking-about look on her face.

"The way we beat them is to *use the rules*," I said. "Since Rita gets to select the location, we select one that'll seat no more than 100 people. The rules say you can open at any time, but you have to close the doors at 7 p.m. George said that of the 200 jobholders, about half are still loyal to y'all, right?"

"That's about right," Rita answered.

"What I envision is that we secure a place that will legally only seat 100 people," I said. "I'll get one of those room-capacity signs you always see in restaurants from the city fire marshal's office. We make sure we have our people sitting in the chairs an hour before the meeting begins. Once the room is filled to capacity, the meeting can officially be closed. Bumstead will be pissed, and I expect he'll appeal to the State Democratic Party. I've checked with them and they told me only two things would close the meeting: The clock and the fire marshal."

63

"I knew I got the right nigger to do this!" George said, getting up to slap my hand.

Rita sat and smiled, shaking her head in agreement.

"There's nothing new about your idea," she said. "My brother told me about a time when he used it."

"What do you think, Ron?" I asked. Ron had been reading something ever since he got there.

"I'm sorry, I have a trial tomorrow," he said. "It's my last case before I quit. Your plan is great. But we've got to make sure we get enough people there early enough to take the seats."

"That, of course, is a key element of the plan that I'm assigning to George and Mrs. Rita. It's crucial that we have all of our people seated one hour before the meeting begins."

"I'll start working on it tonight," Rita said. "I can almost guarantee we'll have our people there."

"Once we get them in there, everything else will be easy," Ron said. "Oh, I forgot to ask: Who are we supporting for president?"

"I was going to support Johnson — until he announced he wasn't going to run again," Rita said. "Now, everything's wide-open. I've been tempted to just go uncommitted."

"I think that's a good idea," Ron said as he put the papers he was reading back into his briefcase. "With the field being as wide-open as it is, going uncommitted will give you more leverage. You can always change later."

"I'm glad you approve, Ron," Rita smiled as she got up. "It's past my bedtime, gentlemen. I'm going to pack it in. When I go to work tomorrow, I'll brief my precinct captains. And I'll contact my people in the police department about a security detail. Some of the people who support Bumstead are some bad actors."

"Well, I've got a date — and she's much prettier than the two of you," I said, gathering my things and walking to the door. "I'll talk to you fellows later."

"Thanks a lot, Billy," George said, shaking my hand with one of the new black-power handshakes. "That shit is going to fuck Bumstead up! He will be fucked up!"

Ron was right behind me. "I've got to prepare for this murder trial in the morning. I'll talk to you tomorrow about a place to hold the caucus."

"That's cool," I said. "I'll be home after 5:30."

***

It was a Thursday night. Janice had to work the next day, so we could not stay out too late. We rented a room at a Holiday Inn in the county. It was the third time we had made out. Janice, ever the blunt one, was direct in saying what was on her mind — and tonight was no exception.

"The sex is great, Billy, but I need to know what your intentions are with me. You know I care about you a lot."

"I want to marry you," I said, realizing this was not the response she expected. "But there are two things I have to do before we get married: I need to pass the state bar exam and get a job."

She leaned over and kissed me. She put her arm around my neck and did not say another word until we got home. When we got to her house, I walked her to the door. When we got to the door, she said, "Yes, I accept your proposal."

The next couple weeks were hectic. I was trying to make sure everything we needed for the caucus was in place. Rita, Ron and

George assured me we would have the people there early. Based on the lack of response from Bumstead when the site for the caucus was announced, it was clear they were totally in the dark about our plans. And surprise was a crucial part of our plan.

On the night of the caucus, everything went "according to Hoyle." More than 150 of our supporters showed up before 6 p.m. Rita's decision to have the police there proved to be a stroke of genius.

When Bumstead's people showed up at 6:30pm, the police enforced the capacity law. We admitted Bumstead and about 10 of his people, but it was standing-room-only. Rita told the police we didn't have any more chairs and we were already over the capacity.

When Bumstead got in and saw what was going on — he started laughing. He knew he had just gotten his ass kicked. He complained loudly to the police, accusing them of conspiring with Rita to prevent his group from participating. The police did not take kindly to his accusations and told him if he did not quiet down, they would put him out. Sensing he had no chance of securing a delegate, Bumstead and his supporters walked out.

Rita then convened the meeting. It ran as smooth as silk and lasted for about an hour. The Ninth Ward was allocated nine delegates, and all went uncommitted. Rita and I were elected delegates, and George was made chairman of the Ninth Ward delegation. When we left the meeting, Bumstead was outside, ranting and raving about how we had screwed him. I told George to take Rita home, and Ron and I got in my car and drove away without acknowledging him. As we drove home to the Southend, Ron began to laugh.

"What's so funny?"

"The look on Bumstead's face when he saw all those people sitting there — and that all the seats were taken. That motherfucker didn't have a clue about what had happened."

"Yeah, I wish I could have seen it," I said.

"And what about you — the man who didn't want to come back to Petersville — who has managed in two months to kick our opponents' asses and decided to marry my cousin!" Ron laughed loudly. "You went and asked Janice to marry you, and you didn't even talk to her cousin, you ace boon-coon! I am really surprised!"

"I didn't know I needed to tell you anything," I said. "Besides, I thought you'd be happy, since my getting married guarantees I'll be around a while."

"Watching you organize that caucus already told me you're going to be around for a while," Ron said. "All bullshit aside, congratulations. I am really very happy for you and Janice."

"Thanks, Brother," I said. "That means you'll be my best man."

"I wouldn't let you ask anyone else," he said. "When is it going to happen?"

"After I pass the bar and get a job."

"You got a job — remember?" he said. "You and I were going to become law partners. All you have to do now is pass the bar. Well, let's find us a bar — and get a drink! We have two things to celebrate: You're getting married and the first ass-kicking for Mr. Bumstead."

CHAPTER 8

Ron and I hung out late that night. We started out at the Panama and ended up at the Living Room. We got drunker than shit. I barely made it home. I told my mother of my plans to get married. I did not tell her of my plan to move out. I still had close to 3k in my savings from Vietnam and I could still draw some unemployment. I decided to get an apartment but keep my voting address in the ninth ward. I surmised that I could study for bar easier in my own apartment and Janice and I would not have to sneak around to motels to make love.

As Rita had predicted having control of 9 uncommitted delegates made her a much sought-after person. The 1968 Democratic Presidential nomination was up for grabs when President Lyndon Johnson bowed out. He had got caught up in the Vietnam quagmire and decided to quit right after he got beat by Senator Eugene McCarthy in the New Hampshire primary. Rita had decided to go with Senator Robert Kennedy. I did not care. I wanted to go to the Democratic National Convention in Chicago as a delegate. The state Democratic Convention was being held in late May. Our nine votes allowed the Kennedy camp to pick up half of the state's delegates. We got three, which meant that Rita, George and I could go.

Although we had been successful with the Caucus, George was still showing some disturbing signs of inattentiveness that were becoming a problem. He was more interested in the glamour and superficial aspect of being a Democratic Committeeman. Whatever Ron or I suggested to him, he ignored. He missed meetings with constituents. The ninth ward was host to three of four major black fraternities and two of the largest black sorority houses were located in the ward.

The largest Prince Hall Mason lodge was also located in the ward. George had become notorious for being late or flat out missing meetings. I had to constantly referee disputes between Ron and him. I had to remind them both who the real enemy was. The last day for candidates to file was May 24th. Our stalking horse was ready and waiting to file. I had met with Mr. Bumstead twice to go over our plan.

He would file at exactly 4:55pm of the 24th. He had a 7:30pm flight to Los Angeles. I was going to pay him $500 a week to take care of his living expenses. In 1968 there were no campaign reporting laws so it was easy to hide the payments. May 24th was on a Monday. That Friday, May 20th, three days before the 24th, Ron, George and I met for breakfast at Hattie's. George was late and looked disoriented. Ron asked him what was wrong and he cursed Ron out and told him to stop fucking with him. He then got up and stormed out of the room. I went after him but could not convince him to stay. When I went back into the dining room, Ron was sitting there with a puzzled look on his face.

"I think George is on something. Have you noticed his mood swings?" I said as I sat back down at the table.

"I don't know what it is, but it is beginning to piss me off. He has gone off on me unnecessarily; for the last time," Ron responded.

"I think I will talk to his mother to see if she has noticed anything."

"Don't go in there calling her son a junkie."

"I know better than to do that."

"Good luck brother, because if he is a junkie we are fucked, because if you and I know, other people know. Speaking of which, I think I will put a call into T.C. He can let me know if there is any street talk about it."

"What's up with T.C. these days? I have not seen him since Vietnam. Did he ever tell you the story about how he and I had a chance meeting in Saigon of my first day in Nam?"

"Yeah he told me."

"Do you talk to him"?

"He hangs out at the Red Rooster, on Madison."

"I guess that is why I have not seen him. Is the Rooster still a dangerous place?"

"Worse, but if you know T.C., nobody is going to fuck with you. I got to get to a meeting with a landlord. I am looking for office space for us."

"That reminds me I got an appointment also in the Old Town district. I am looking for an apartment."

"You had better be prepared to sue. Those honkies don't want to rent to black people. Some of them even have signs in their windows that still say "whites only."

"That is the nicest section of the 9th ward. And if I think that I have been denied the right to rent any apartment by any landlord, I *will* sue them."

I left Ron at Hattie's and went to pick up Janice. It made no sense to rent an apartment without her input since I envisioned her spending a lot of time there before and after we get married. Most of the landlords were polite. Ironically, we found this apartment building owned by this Jewish man married to a black woman. As he showed us the apartment he talked about how happy he was that a black person was trying to move in Old Town. Most blacks avoid this area when they are looking for an apartment. He told me that the Old Town area had changed. A number of college students had moved there over the years, which had help to make the climate more civil.

The apartment he showed us was a large two-bedroom unit with ten-foot ceilings and wooden floors. The owner had modernized in with a new kitchen and bathroom. Janice and I fell in love with it and the neighborhood. It was close to the university that Janice attended at night, which of course, helped sell us on it. I filled out all the necessary forms and put a deposit down to hold it. Afterwards we decided to have lunch at a small deli next door. There were a number of little quaint shops that reminded me of the Georgetown section of D.C. After eating Janice and I left to go home.

I had decided to stop by my house first to talk to my mother and tell her about my plans to get married. As I pulled on to my block, I saw several police cars parked in front of George's house. As I got closer I saw an ambulance and a body lying in a pool of blood. I pulled over and Janice and I got out of the car.

"Billy," a familiar voice called to me from behind. It was Meat. "George has been killed. He was shot in the head."

I looked over to the front of George's house and saw my mother going in to see Rita. I started walking over to where George's body was laid. A policeman put his arm up to stop me, but Meat interrupted and told him I was family. *Who the fuck wanted to kill George? Bumstead? The Lebanese?* I thought to myself. I grabbed Janice by the hand and walked up to the house. My mother was sitting on the couch with Rita.

When Rita saw me she jumped and shouted. "They killed my boy, Billy! They killed my boy! That goddam Bumstead and the

Lebanese killed my boy!" She was crying and screaming uncontrollably. Modear said she had called Dr. Madison.

Good old Dr. Madison's office was two doors down from Rita's house. He had been in the neighborhood for 30 years. While she was trying to calm Rita down, Dr. Madison came in and gave her something in glass.

At that moment, Ron walked through the door. Rita started crying just as loud as she had before. Ron and George had grown up together and were like brothers.

"This can't be true," Ron said looking and Meat. "How did it happen?"

"Someone with a high-powered rifle, shot him from a distance. That is all I can tell you until the police complete their investigation."

Ron stopped asking Meat questions. He knew the routine. Ron walked over and embraced Rita. Whatever Dr. Madison gave her was not working yet. I grabbed Ron's arm and pulled him aside so my mother and Janice could set her down. I slowly coaxed Ron into the kitchen.

"What the fuck is going on Ron? Do you think Bumstead and the Lebanese are that fucking desperate?" I asked.

"There is only one major benefactor of George's demise and that is Bumstead and his supporters, the Lebanese." Ron cried. Tears were rolling down his face as he started screaming hysterically. "It is nothing more than a goddamn political assassination."

"Calm down man. If this is what you say it is, then we have got to think fast. Rita is going to be out of it for a while. If it was the Lebanese and Bumstead, then we have to make some decisions real soon."

"Why do you keep saying *if*? What happened tonight is clear to me." Ron responded with his eyebrows raised to show how incredulously he thought about what I was saying.

"You and I both commented on how strange George was acting this morning. Maybe something else was going on his life that we don't know about," I answered, realizing that my comments were not going to change his mind or anyone else's.

"Fuck that being a lawyer shit right now Billy. These motherfuckers did the same thing to one of their own two years ago under the same circumstances. They settle their political problems the same way they settle all their problems. We should have known that if they would kill one of their own, a nigger would not mean shit to them," Ron said angrily.

I decided to leave that conversation alone. What was important now was to try and help Rita cope with losing her only child. I kept Ron in the kitchen until he had calmed down. When we walked back into the room, Ron went over to the couch to talk to Rita. I went back outside to talk to Meat.

The word of the shooting had spread fast. Word of mouth through the telephone was still the most reliable information dissemination method of choice in the Southend. A small crowd had gathered outside. Most of them were neighborhood people who were curious about what had happened. When I got out the door, Meat motioned to me to come over to the side of the house. I walked over to the gangway on the south side of the house and stood there for about three minutes before he walked over to where I was.

"The preliminary analysis says George was shot at long range in the head. He died instantly," Meat reported.

"I know the answer to this question before I am asking it, but is there any clue as to who it was?" I asked.

"I overheard one of the homicide dicks saying the bullet was very similar to the one that killed Victor Lietibe last year."

"Ron said something very similar. I was in Vietnam when that happened. What was it all about?"

"Lietibe was the committeeman of the 12th ward. According to Police department intelligence, the 12th ward is one of the wards that the Lebanese crime syndicate controls. It borders the river like the 9th Ward does. Lietibe was not Lebanese but had married into the family of Ansur Thomas, the person who most people identify as the head of the Lebanese crime organization. His wife died of cancer about a year ago and Lietibe began to exhibit signs of possibly breaking away from the Lebanese. In December of 1967, he was shot in the head with a high-powered rifle of what looks like the same caliber. Other than that, we don't have anything that could get us even a conversation with the prosecutor. I have got to go now, if I hear anything I will get in touch."

I shook Meat's hand and walked back inside. Ron's theory was gaining momentum. But to what end? This was a clean killing with very few clues. It was also professionally done. I walked over to Janice and motioned for her to come to me.

"It is late; I can take you home if you like?" I asked.

"Rita told your mother George's shooting was a professional hit. Does that mean that you and Ron might be in some type of danger?" Janice queried me with her voice trembling with anxiety.

"I don't know baby. Your guess is as good as mine," I answered unsatisfactorily.

"That is not an answer," Janice responded angrily.

"That is the best answer I can give. You are going to have to ask those people who killed them what their plans are for Ron and I."

I embraced her to let her know that I understood her question; I just did not have an answer.

"I am going to go back in the house to talk to Ron for a minute and then we are going to leave." She nodded in agreement and walked over to the porch and sat down on an old metal lawn chair. I went back in the room to tell Ron what Meat had told me about the possible Lebanese link. It was almost 8pm. Ron told me he needed to meet with me later to talk. I told him that I had to take Janice home and would meet him if front of my house between 9:30 and 10:00. He agreed. I then went to say goodbye to Rita. The effects of whatever Dr. Madison had given her was finally working. She was lying in her bed asleep.

My mother stopped me at the door to tell me that she had decided to stay with Rita that evening to keep her from having to spend the night in her house alone. In less than a year Rita had lost her only brother and her only child.

Taking Janice home and leaving her was not as easy as I told Ron it would be. She had insisted of staying with me for the rest of the night. When I met Ron, I told him we were a threesome that night. His face registered a sign of protest, but he did not say anything. He suggested that we go to dinner. I was not excited about eating that late, but I was more interested in his mental state, so I said ok. Since my car was a two-seater, we had to ride in his mustang. Ron took us to a place in the Old Town section called O'Leary's. It was a hangout for all the so-called white progressives and the pseudo hippies in Petersville.

O'Leary's was famous for its hamburgers, roast beef sandwiches and cold beer. This was before all the white progressives stopped eating red meat and became animal activists. Most of them were the whites that saw the civil rights movement as some kind of out-of-body experience. We were the only blacks in the place on this Friday night. Ron asked for and got a booth in the back. I assumed it was to give us some privacy while we talked. After the waitress took our order, Ron started talking incessantly. I thought he wanted to reminisce about George, but in typical Ron Jackson, he started to spell out a plan of action to continue the campaign.

"This can be an opportunity for us Billy," Ron said sipping his beer and sitting it back on the table. "You and I both know that George was slipping and sliding all over the place. I love and will miss him as a friend, but he was going to make a lousy committeeman."

"Don't try to sound too remorseful," Janice reacted with a sarcastic laugh.

"I know this sounds cold, but it does not have to change our ultimate strategy for gaining control of the ninth ward."

"How can you do that without George? I asked.

"George did not have any politics. His politics were me and his mother."

"Notwithstanding that what you are saying might be accurate, George was the candidate. He was the horse we were riding."

"And I am proposing that we get us a new horse. What do you think about me filing for Committeeman?"

"You got a death wish?" Janice blurted out.

"No. But I would rather that if it was my time to go, I would want to go down fighting for something I believe in than to die as a superfluous entity that was born, lived and died," Ron shot back.

76

"Filing is one thing, winning is everything. That is the only question I have. If half of Connors' people defected from Rita when he died, how many do you think will stay now?"

"I think a lot of them will stay once they hear my message. We can turn George's death into a battle cry of political freedom. George can be a martyr that we can use to talk about reforming the patronage system. I had even thought about changing the name of the 9th Ward Democratic Club to the George Martin Democratic Organization."

"Don't you think you need to talk to Rita? She might not see this the same way you do," Janice interrupted.

"That is not a bad idea Ron," I added. "But however good your intentions, this could be seen as just blind ambition on your part and in bad taste."

"All Rita is thinking about right now is her son and that is all she *should* be thinking of. Someone has to step up to the plate and make sure the perpetrators of this foul deed are not successful. The best revenge we can have is to keep the organization in-tact. Besides, what have I got to lose?"

"It looks like your life. You seem to be taking a very cavalier attitude towards what happened tonight. Whoever you are talking about is serious about holding onto what they perceive to be theirs," Janice said.

"I am not being cavalier; I am serious. If Bumstead and the Lebanese are behind this, we cannot let them succeed through intimidation. The Lebanese see an opportunity to get a foothold in another river ward. They had a relationship with Connors, but it was based on a quid pro quo. With Bumstead they would have total control."

"Ron is right Janice. If we are going to be participants in the process, we must draw a line somewhere. The thugs who killed

George are no different than the rednecks that killed Medgar Evers, Martin Luther King Jr. or Emmitt Till. They did it for the same reason, white is right and black has to get back," I added.

"Are you all sure this is not just some macho bullshit, you kill my cat I shoot your dog?" Janice responded.

"It might be, which is a far sight better than you kill my dog and I run and hide," I answered.

"You and Ron both know I will support whatever you do. I just want to make sure that y'all understand what's at stake," Janice responded.

"Our future, our children's future," Ron said reaching across the table to touch Janice's hand. The waitress was back with our food. "Come on and let's eat our food before it gets cold."

We continued to talk about when he would file and whether he should tell Rita. We concluded that although telling her now would be perceived as being in poor taste, it was crucial to tell her. She might be pissed off if you tell her, but she will be more than pissed off if she hears it from someone else and feels she was blindsided. Besides, unless the funeral was going to be held before Tuesday, she was going to find out. We would just have to risk that Rita would not be mad too long. Ron decided to tell her Sunday after church.

CHAPTER 9

Ron and I spent the next day at Rita's house. Try as we could, she was understandably inconsolable. I spent the day helping with the funeral arrangements. Black's funeral home was still operating; in fact, Rita was the owner, making the arrangement process seamless.

That evening I spent some quiet time with Janice trying to ensure her that Ron and I were ok. Of course, she did not buy any of my arguments. Frustrated, I took her home at 9pm. We both agreed that we would need to try and get some sleep because church service in the morning was going to be tough.

In his sermon that morning, Janice's father talked about George's murder. He all but accused the Syrians of killing George in an attempt to select our leaders. Janice looked at me and smiled when he talked about how the Southend community had to throw the yoke of slavery off our necks and elect our own leaders — not someone handpicked by outsiders. Supporters of Bumstead, sensing that Rev Jackson was talking about them, walked out during his sermon.

When we were walking out of the church, Ron said he tried to talk to Rita, but she was still upset. He decided, and I concurred, that he should go downtown to the Petersville Election Board and file as soon as it opened Monday. The more I thought about it, I concluded that Bumstead would be pressuring Rita, trying to get her to cut a deal with him. He would, of course, deny that he had anything to do with George's death. With Ron filing, this would give her some time to decide on an option. It would provide an element of surprise. And we still had our secret weapon — the stalking horse.

Ron filed at precisely 8am Monday morning and we both went to Rita's house. When we arrived, she seated us at her table for breakfast and discussion.

"Who wants coffee?" she asked. "Y'all have been busy this morning, I hear," she said, standing at the stove with her back to us.

"We wanted to tell you yesterday, Mrs. Martin, but did not know how," Ron stammered. "We just thought somebody ought to file as a precaution. I'm prepared to withdraw, if you want me to."

"You know who called and told me, don't you?"

"Bumstead?" I answered.

"He offered me a deal," she said. "He told me he didn't have anything to do with George's murder, that if he and I could team up, nobody could beat us. He also said you and Billy were ambitious and young — and should sit down and wait your turn."

Ron and I were speechless. There was really nothing we could say. After about 30 seconds, Ron broke the silence. He stood and walked over to the coffeepot. He poured himself another cup, turned and stood by the counter.

"It all boils down to who you trust, Mrs. Martin. Bumstead — whether or not he had something to do with George's shooting — owes his soul to the Syrians. We owe our souls to you and to the Southend. It won't have any direct impact on you economically whom you choose. You will have a job and the house and other assets. Billy and I need you. You don't need us."

"Stop right now," she said, motioning us to sit. "I'm not going to cut a deal with the people who killed my son! I might cut one of them." She lifted a skillet filled with scrambled eggs and walked over to table.

"I could never trust Bumstead, and I might not be able to trust y'all. My brother came to power in a different time and different place. He cut deals and made alliances with the Syrians and others because he believed he had to. I didn't always agree with him, but he was my brother and I trusted what he was doing, what he thought was best for his family and for the Southend. Remember, for a long time he was the only black elected official in Petersville. I have already called the chairman of City Democratic Central Committee and told him I'm going to put your name up for nomination to replace George. That way, you can run as an incumbent.

"I understand how and why you felt you had to file this morning, even though you didn't consult me. I was my brother's committeewoman for 15 years. I had to put up with his not consulting me. But I am not going to tolerate it from you. You understand?"

"Yes ma'am, it won't happen again," Ron answered.

"Good," Rita said. "Now eat your food. I've got to go to the funeral home. Billy's momma is picking me up in a few minutes. We will talk again on Friday. The funeral is Wednesday and I don't think I'll be ready to talk until then." She was wiping tears from her eyes.

I felt selfish about the entire process, but I was with Ron, who knew how to quickly bring you back to his reality. Rita's response was obviously better than either of us could have anticipated. Ron's plan had been advanced at least four years. He was riding his own horse now, instead of having to use George as a surrogate. The next big step was implementing our secret weapon. It was important that after filing our stalking horse, we got him to the airport and on the plane to Los Angeles before anyone got a chance to talk to him. I hired someone to pick him up at home, drive him to election board to file and then to the airport. Only Ron and I would know how to contact him.

It was ironic that George's wake Tuesday evening was scheduled the same day we filed our stalking horse. Almost every elected official in Petersville was there to pay his or her respects to Rita — even Bumstead. He was standing at the sign-in register when Ron, Janice and I walked in. A man standing behind him nudged him in the back to get his attention. Bumstead turned and, upon seeing Ron, walked straight toward us. His high-yellow face had turned ruby-red with anger and sweat was bouncing off him like a waterfall hitting rocks below it. Bumstead had been an amateur boxer and years ago had been one of Mr. Connors' enforcers. He had long since lost his boxer physique and was now just a three-hundred-pound overweight bully. He was a deputy sheriff now and could legally carry a gun, a thought that made me extremely nervous as he moved toward us. He got right in Ron's face and started cursing.

"You little punk-ass motherfucker," he growled. "You don't have a clue who you fucking with! That little game you played today — filing that other candidate — won't work. I'm going to find him and kick your ass *and* his ass if he don't withdraw!"

Ron leaned over and whispered to Bumstead, "This is not the time or place to talk about this. Call me in the morning and I'll meet you and talk about it. But for now, you need to get the fuck out of my face and get your fat ass out of my way."

Bumstead lost it. He cocked his arm to strike Ron. Out of nowhere came another arm that put Bumstead in an abbreviated half-nelson and pushed him out the door. Ron and I watched as

Bumstead stumbled down the steps and onto the sidewalk. The mysterious stranger maintained his hold.

"Whoever you are, when you let me go, I'm going to fuck you up!" Bumstead yelled.

"Then I better not let you go, motherfucker," the mystery man said.

One of Bumstead's friends came running outside. "Let me talk to him, my man."

"Okay, 'cause I ain't lettin' him go till he cools out."

"You need to calm down, Bum."

"Fuck you, I need this punk to let me go," Bumstead protested.

"The punk you're referring to is Teddy Chambers."

"Shit," Bumstead nervously stuttered. "This isn't about you, T.C. I didn't know it was you."

T.C. released his hold.

"Why would you want to start some shit at George's wake?" he said. "You couldn't wait till George's people left?"

"I just got pissed off at that little sissy for trying to fuck with my politics!" Bumstead shouted, pointing at Ron.

"That 'little sissy' you're referring to is a personal friend of mine," T.C. said. "I consider him almost as close as a brother. If anything happens to him, I will be *very* pissed off!"

Bumstead massaged his arm. "I'll see you at the ballot box. That ringer you put in won't mean shit," he said, backing away from T.C.

"Now that's the civilized way to settle conflict, but I can give you either one," T.C. laughed.

I had not seen T.C. since I had returned home. He still looked good, but you could see the advanced age in his coal-black eyes. I walked up to him and we embraced. I felt the cold steel against my ribs.

"It's good to see you," I blurted out, trying to change the subject. "We need to go inside and see Mrs. Martin."

"I have already seen her."

"How can I get in touch with you?" I asked. "I haven't seen you since Vietnam."

"I live on Maple Road. Ron has my number. I got to go see a man about a dog," T.C. said, and he walked away.

Inside, everyone was talking about how T.C. had checked Bumstead. Some of Bumstead's workers asked Ron and me if they could rejoin the organization. They were upset about what happened to George, and Bumstead's behavior tonight was the last straw.

The funeral was an emotionally wrenching experience. I remembered all the arguments I had with George and wished I had let him win more of them. Both Ron and I couldn't help but follow suit when we saw Rita crying.

***

The Petersville Democratic Central Committee was scheduled to meet the next Tuesday. Rita already had put on the agenda Ron's appointment as Ninth Ward Democratic committeeman. She told me that, although the Syrians and several black committee people were dead-set against Ron getting the appointment, a majority of the committee members had assured her they would not go against party tradition. The surviving committee person always had been allowed to choose the successor until the next election.

The Syrians, however, were known to use money, drugs, sex and whatever else to buy votes — so nothing could be taken for granted. Rita was checking her traps, making phone calls until the last few minutes before the meeting began. The vote was 24-12. The Syrians picked up six votes from the three wards they controlled, four from the other two black wards and two from the 14th Ward.

Immediately after the vote, Ron resigned from his job in the public defender's office. He could not hold an elective office and be employed by the public defender.

Ron didn't allow any dust to settle before he started working. The first thing he did was schedule a special ward meeting — open to the public — for a week from the day he was appointed.

He had convinced Rita they needed a new approach to getting people interested in politics. Most ward organizations did not publicize their meetings. They would inform only the patronage workers about the meeting times and locations. Ron and I had tried to convince George to open the meetings and democratize the process, but he was afraid he would lose control. Rita's initial response was the same. We had to spend all night convincing her the way to beat Bumstead — and to keep the Syrians from stealing from the ballot box — was to make sure there was a massive voter turnout.

Ron and I were putting a system in place that we could replicate in future elections. We got Rita to agree to the drafting of a set of bylaws that would make the organization more democratic.

We started by changing the organization's name to the George Martin Ninth Ward Democratic Organization. It was a strategic move to garner sympathy from voters. Initially, Rita was reluctant, but she understood the importance of winning.

I was responsible for writing a rough draft of the new bylaws, which included allowing members to vote on endorsements. The new rules established an executive board that made recommendations, but the entire membership would ratify the recommendations. Annual membership dues were established and the patronage workers' one percent salary assessment was eliminated. However, they still had to work for free on election days.

More than 300 people attended our first meeting, held in the basement of St. Mark's Church. No one could remember when a Democratic ward organization had operated as a democracy. Someone tipped the press, and there was a little blurb in the newspaper about our meeting.

But the important thing was the imprint the meeting left on Rita. Many people she had never seen attended that first ward meeting. More than 250 paid the $2 membership dues. Most of them not only had been apolitical — they had never even voted.

Ron's plan was to create a new base of support in the ward instead of trying to build one with the existing members of the Ninth Ward organization. A large percentage of the new people were our peers. All were issued cards. Ron was elected the temporary chairman until the new bylaws were written and approved. A bylaws committee was selected and given two months to work on them before reporting back to the full body. Ron made me chairman of the committee. Rita did not say a lot but she sensed something different was happening.

At the end of the meeting, which lasted less than an hour, I reminded everyone there was an election in less than two months. I asked them to volunteer and to become block captains. I gave them information on how to organize their blocks.

The campaign was geared to target the non-traditional voter. I had researched the voting patterns of the registered voters of the

Ninth Ward, which revealed more than 70 percent of the black registered voters had participated in the November 1964 presidential election. This was in sharp contrast to the 45 percent turnout for the August 1964 primary election. Developing an organization that could deliver a vote was an essential first test for us.

Our next test was the selection of delegates for the Democratic National Convention scheduled for August in Chicago. Rita, Ron and I wanted to go, but we didn't think we could get the votes to leverage three delegates. Because of Rita's seniority as a Democratic Party official — and out of sympathy for George's death — she was able to get the State Democratic Party to appoint her as an at-large delegate. This left us free to leverage our votes for two delegates at the state convention, which was set for the third Saturday in June at the state capital.

The party leadership wanted to support Hubert Humphrey. This was fortunate for us because our votes became crucial in shutting out the other candidate's supporters' ability to meet the threshold for a viable caucus. We were rewarded with two delegates.

We stayed committed to Robert Kennedy until Sirhan Sirhan assassinated him on June 6, 1968, the night he won the California Presidential Primary. The sequence of events since I returned from Vietnam was beginning to really make me weary. Martin Luther King, George and now Robert Kennedy? What the fuck was going on?

The 1968 Democratic National Convention in Chicago was the beginning of the end for all who thought the revolution was just around the corner. The assassination of Martin Luther King Jr. and presidential candidate Robert Kennedy were the warning shots from people who were tired of our generation's attempts to bring about change.

Ron and I stayed at the Drake Hotel. I was fascinated by the grandeur of the Drake. The United Auto Workers Union, which took care of our expenses, was a strong supporter of Hubert Humphrey and wanted to make sure that every delegate committed to him got to Chicago — and was properly cared for. When I told the political action coordinator the cost of staying at the Drake, his eyebrow rose, but he didn't say no.

Ron, Janice and I were in our room, trying to decide whether to go to dinner or to a large, anti-war rally in Grant Park. I told Ron I had heard rumors the anti-war people were going to try to crash the gate at the convention.

"That's what the police and that fascist Mayor Richard Daley want the public to believe," he responded, sipping the complimentary champagne the UAW had sent to the room. "It'll give him an excuse to brutalize them. I heard a bunch of cops beat some protesters in Lincoln Park last night."

"Well, I'm not going to make myself cannon fodder for Chicago's finest," I said. "I'm taking my woman out to dinner. You ought to go with us. I made reservations at Rick's Fish Market. A guy from Chicago named Reginald Valentine who I met in Vietnam told me if I ever got to Chicago, I had to check out Rick's."

I had seen the way the police had handled the demonstrations in San Francisco and Berkeley, so I was not going to deliberately put myself in harm's way. Ron had already made up his mind to go, so nothing I said was going to change it.

Our dinner reservation was for 8 pm and the restaurant was a 10-minute cab ride from the Drake. Janice and I got dressed and left Ron at the hotel.

Valentine did not lie about Rick's. The food, service and ambiance were excellent. Janice and I drank a bottle of champagne to formally toast our engagement. When we got back to the hotel, the lobby was crowded with people — some bleeding, others wrapped in bandages. All were crying and talking about what had happened at the anti-war demonstration. It was precisely what I predicted. The Chicago police beat the cowboy shit out of the protesters. I called Ron's room to see if he made it back. He answered the phone and told us to come up.

"Those white policemen beat those white kids like they were niggers," he laughed. "I never thought I would see the day that white police would beat up on white kids like that. I know, I know, you told me — but I had to see it myself."

"Did you go to Grant Park?" I asked.

"I went down there for a few minutes," he said. "When I saw this army of Chicago cops, I decided to come back here. The police told them to stay in the park. When the crowd started marching towards the convention hall, the police began whippin' heads. The police were everywhere. They even hit reporters — anybody within the length of their nightsticks. This is going to look real bad on TV for the Democrats. It could make them lose in November."

"With all the hippies either in the hospital or in jail, Rush Street ought to be quiet," I said. "Jan and I were going to go bar-hopping. Come on and go with us."

"That's cool with me," Ron said.

The convention was a dogfight. Robert Kennedy's assassination in June on the night of the California Presidential Primary had thrown everything into a tailspin. Johnson's vice president, former Minnesota Senator Hubert Humphrey, was being sold as the brokered candidate. Most of our state delegation supported Humphrey — except for a few of us who wanted to see Senator Eugene McCarthy in the White House. Humphrey was nominated, but the Democratic Party was severely divided.

CHAPTER 10

As hard as we tried, Ron and I could not get excited or focused about the convention, so two days before it ended, we decided to go home.

We had to get back to Petersville to work our own election. The convention was held in July, only three weeks before the primary. With all three of us gone, Ron, Rita and I had to rely on others to keep things going. Rita was unopposed, so she could afford to stay in Chicago, but we had to beat Bumstead. When we got home, we found very little of what had to be done was completed.

I had ordered the printing of 30,000 campaign brochures, which were supposed to be stuffed into envelopes along with brochures for candidates for governor and U.S. senator. After being stuffed, they were supposed to be bundled and taken to the post for mailing. The candidates for governor and the senator had paid for the postage and envelope printing. The people assigned and paid to do this had stuffed only 3,000 envelopes in two days. In our naiveté, Ron and I initially thought we could get the work done by using volunteers.

We had enough volunteers scheduled so the task could have been completed in a day. Unfortunately, the number of volunteers scheduled did not show up. I learned a valuable lesson about running a campaign: You needed money to win.

The problem with volunteers is they are on their own time — not yours. And to get them motivated to work on your time, you had to pay them. Once we got back and I hired people to work, things got done. I had recruited some friends for door-to-door canvassing. Fifty people showed up the first weekend, but only 15 the following weekends. After realizing how undependable volunteers can be, I put out a message on the street that we were paying campaign workers $2 an hour. More than 100 people soon showed up at our headquarters.

Fortunately, an old-money patriarch whose real name was Richard Honest Smith — wanted to run for governor. He had inherited money from his family, investment bankers who had helped finance the transcontinental railroad. Smith had lived in New York for the past 20 years but decided to move back home in 1968 to run for governor.

Smith decided to use his middle and last names when he filed for governor to allow his name to appear on the ballot as Honest Smith. Honest Smith's strategy was to collect as many endorsements as his family's money could buy.

When he began meeting with various elected officials and asking how much money they would need to endorse him, a feeding-frenzy began. Wallace Allen, the 11th Ward Democratic committeeman, said he could get Smith the endorsements of every elected black official in the Southend for $100,000. Smith had his lawyer give Allen $50,000 in cash on the spot. The rest would come when Allen produced the endorsements.

Allen left the meeting and went straight to Rita's house. He said he had to see us immediately. Ron, Rita, Allen and I went into Rita's bedroom, where he showed us the money and told us the story. He said he would give us $5,000 for a letter of endorsement. Rita said we already had decided to endorse the incumbent. I quickly pulled Rita into the hall and told her this money was almost twice what we needed to run a successful campaign.

Allen was yelling at us from the bedroom.

"I know you've already committed to Tom Easton. I don't want you to change. I'm going to use the letter 'just for show.' Then I'm going to double-cross Smith. I saw all this money, and I just couldn't leave it on the table."

Rita suggested a plan she had seen her brother use years ago. She would endorse Easton — but Ron would endorse Smith. That way, both candidates could claim they had the Ninth Ward's endorsement. That was fine with Allen. All he wanted was a letter from the Ninth Ward endorsing Smith in the primary.

In 1968, there were no campaign-finance laws that restricted how much money a candidate could collect or spend. Neither were there any reporting requirements. Monies could be used for personal expenses as long as the income was reported to the Internal Revenue Service. Years later, Allen told me he bought a house with $35,000 of the money Smith gave him.

On Election Day, Rita overwhelmingly won the committeewoman's seat over Bumstead's running mate. Her huge margin helped Ron squeeze past Bumstead by a margin of only 2 percent. The stalking-horse candidate got 8 percent, splitting the vote exactly the way we had hoped.

The victory party was held at The Panama. We partied until my mother put us out. After taking Rita and Janice home, Ron and I went to my house to have our own private toast. Ron had bought a bottle of cognac.

"Here's to the successful completion of Phase One," Ron said, raising his glass to mine.

"Cheers," I responded — and felt the heat of the cognac ignite my throat.

"Which elective office has the most impact on black people in this town?" Ron asked and poured us another drink.

I hesitated at being surprised by the question. "The mayor's? Don't tell me you're thinking about running for mayor?!"

Ron handed me another drink and sat down.

"You're wrong. The man who has the most impact is the one who can charge you with a crime and put you in jail — and that is the prosecutor."

"I agree, but what's your point?"

"I'm going to run for district attorney."

"Shit, Ron! Now I'm convinced you've gone crazy! Harry Johnson is unbeatable — and he is vindictive. He ran unopposed in the last two elections. He'll come down on you like a ton of bricks when he finds out you want to fuck with him."

"Everything you say about Johnson is correct," Ron said. "He's a formidable foe and it'll be hard to take down — but not impossible.

"Last year this time, no one would have predicted that Black Connors would be dead and I'd be his replacement. We would upset the political equation in this town something fierce if we could capture the district attorney's office."

"We could also effectively end our political and legal careers if we take a shot at Johnson — and miss," I said, pouring myself another glass of cognac.

"But we're not going to lose," Ron said. "As a matter of fact, Johnson is not going to file for re-election."

"Aw, bullshit," I growled. "He's already made his announcement."

"I didn't say he was not going to announce," Ron said, giving off that sneaky grin he was always trying to disguise. "I said he was not going to run."

"You're playing with fire — and getting burned is not the worst thing that could happen to you!" I warned.

"I'm not going to talk to you about the details. I just wanted you to know my plans."

"You are the strongest motherfucker I know, man!" I laughed, shooting down another drink in the process.

"You haven't been sworn in as committeeman yet, and already you're talking about taking on one of the baddest motherfuckin' white boys in Petersville."

"You're only looking at the negatives," Ron said. "When I win, I'll hire you as my top assistant. We'll be able to hire a cadre of black lawyers who will become the nucleus of a dynamic political organization. The prosecutor's office can become an incubator of black leadership. We could groom potential candidates for the school board, state representatives, the city council, the mayor, the U.S. Congress. Man, the sky is the limit!"

It was difficult to decipher between being impressed and scared to death at the same time. We talked until almost 6am. Ron had a clear, cogent and focused understanding about what he was going to do. And he had worn me down. I stopped arguing and just listened for the rest of the time. We drank the whole bottle of cognac before we both crashed on the couch.

We slept until the phone woke us up at 9am. It was Janice, calling from work to remind me about a state bar-exam review class I had signed up for — and it would start in exactly one hour. I had originally planned to take the bar exam in June but decided to postpone it until October, after the campaign. I woke Ron, took two aspirin, dressed and rushed out to the class. I had to get a job, and passing the bar was essential to that end.

Ron got up and began making phone calls to congratulate all the candidates who had won their respective races. As I rushed out the door, he gave me a fast wink. He knew exactly what he was doing.

CHAPTER 11

The review class was I exactly what I needed. I graduated from law school two years ago and passed the bar on my first try. In 1968 black lawyers were rare and passing the bar on your first try was even more unusual for a black person. Ron was impressed at my ability to take the bar exam and pass given all of the distractions I had to deal with this year that he suggested I should start a business giving seminars on how to pass the bar.

I immediately joined the law firm that Ron had organized. Although my specialty was contract law, there was very little demand for a black corporate lawyer in Petersville. In fact, there were only 25 black lawyers in town and all of those who were in private practice, practiced criminal law. We rented an office in Old Town, directly across from my apartment. Being close made it easy to get to work, but it had very little impact on making money. Most of our clients were poor otherwise why would they be fooling with us? Most blacks were reluctant to deal with black lawyers because they perceived that the black lawyers could not get anything done. When all you saw were white judges and only one black lawyer in the prosecutors' office (and he was harder on blacks than the whites were) you could understand why they felt that way. White lawyers had the relationships and could cut the deals, for a fee. They, the white assistant prosecuting attorneys and the defense attorneys, all knew each other from the good old boy network from law school, socially, high school or the country club. I quickly learned that the only people who should go to law school are those whose father owns a law firm.

My initial experience in the courts with my clients who were poor and black helped me see what Ron meant when he said that the DA was the most powerful person in government. I was still unconvinced that he could defeat the DA, Harry Johnson. His running had the potential if he lost, of making it harder for us to have any success in the Petersville judicial system.

Many of my clients and other blacks that had got caught in the judicial system should have never been there. Blacks were routinely charged with crimes while whites were given the benefit of the doubt. I used to go to the night or weekend warrant desk to hawk cases and was witness to the uneven use of prosecutorial discretion by the prosecutor assigned to the night watch. Unless a white person had committed murder of some type of major felony, he was released routinely without a bail requirement. I *never* saw a black receive a release without a bail over a six-month period that I observed the night warrant's desk. Whites would make an argument that they needed to be released to go to work as an argument to support their case for release. Blacks were locked up until Monday when they could be arraigned. This meant that if they had a job, they were going to be late or absent to the job.

May 24th was the day filing for the Democratic Primary in August opened and Ron did what he said he was going to do: He filed to seek the office of District Attorney. I still did not believe he actually did it. He filed the moment the office opened. Ron was the first person to file and because Johnson had been unopposed in the last two elections and his filing made the front page of the daily newspaper. When asked about Ron's filing against him, Johnson referred to Ron as a nuisance. Ron and I had scheduled lunch at Flannigan's Pub in Old Town near our office that same day. When I told him what Johnson said about him in the newspaper he laughed.

Taking a huge bite out his hamburger, Ron continued to chuckle. "He does not realize just what kind of nuisance I really am."

"I am going to be with you Ron, no matter what, but I swear I don't understand how you are going to win. Bumstead and his supporters have already been campaigning to recapture the Committeeman's post and the Syrians are going to throw everything but the kitchen sink at us. I thought we would work on consolidating our base before running for another office."

"You make some good points, I just don't think we should be predictable. Besides there is a strong possibility that Johnson may not stand for re-election."

"Why do you keep saying that? Do you know something that no one else knows?"

"Don't worry about what I know, you will know everything you need to know at the appropriate time. Hurry up and finish eating. I have got to be back in court at 2:30 this afternoon. I am representing T.C. on a case that is getting ready to get thrown out of court."

"This is the third time in three months that you have been on a case involving T.C. His initials must stand for trouble coming instead of Teddy Chambers," I said hoping to get a laugh.

"The T.C. stands for timely and in cash. He pays big and he pays on time," Ron snarled back.

I immediately knew to change the subject because my clients had bigger problems than T.C.'s and they did not pay. I got the message from Ron. T.C. was a paying client as opposed to one of my non-paying ones.

***

The next weekend was the Memorial Day holiday and I decided to have a cookout and open house at my new apartment to celebrate passing the bar. The weather forecast had predicted that the temperature was going to be in the 90's. I had small barbecue pit that I put on a small patio that overlooked the street.

It was a little after 7am when I saw Ron and someone going into the office. I was standing in the living room looking out the patio door, so Ron could not see me behind the curtains.

I had told everyone to come over after 4pm. Since Ron was already at his office, he got there early. Janice had also came over early that morning to make potato salad, spaghetti, coleslaw and baked beans. As was the custom with Ron, very few things were coincidental. He had a case of Coors beer with him when he finally came up the stairs.

"One of clients brought this back from Denver for me. I thought I would bring it over to liven up your party."

"Thank you, Ron. It's not stolen is it? Is that the same client you were meeting with this morning?"

"I did not think anyone saw me that early on a holiday."

"You got caught"

"Hi Jan, have you been home girl?" Ron laughed.

Janice did not turn around to acknowledge Ron.

Ron took the beer into the kitchen and put it in a cooler I had sitting on the floor. He put all the beer in the cooler except for two cans that he brought back out to the patio.

"That client you saw this morning brought in the last piece I need to win the election for DA," he said as he handed me a beer. He then pulled the wooden patio door shut.

"The client you saw this morning is the biggest pimp in Petersville. I am handling a case he got in Colorado. Although

100

everyone including the police knows who and what he is, he has never been charged with *anything* in Petersville."

"You started out by saying that this client was the key to you winning the DA's election. Is there a connection here?"

"Patience my friend, you have got to hear the whole story to appreciate it. About six months ago my client got busted for procurement of prostitution and possession of heroin. He called me and had me arrange a bond for him. The normal bond for a case like this is 25K. The prosecutor got the Judge to set the bond at $2500. I asked my client why and he told me that he had a thing on Harry Johnson. I asked him what kind of thing. His reply? I *am* one of his pimps."

I turned to look at Ron and my hand knocked my water bottle over.

"Get the fuck out of here."

"Straight up. That's what he said. I even tested his power over Johnson. I had a young male client who had been arrested for possession of a controlled substance and armed criminal action and his bond was set at twenty-five thousand dollars cash bond. I asked Johnson's pimp if he could get my client's bond reduced. Two days later, the DA reduced the bond to $5,000."

"That is still hard to believe that someone so straight-laced as Johnson would let someone get into him like that."

"My client says that Johnson is a serious sex fiend. He claims that he has supplied Johnson with girls on more than one occasion. To keep from being set up, Johnson used different pimps each time he went on a foray. He usually ventured out once a month."

"This shit is crazy. Don't tell me you are going to try and use this against Johnson? If the answer is yes, you *do* know that you are fucking with some dangerous shit."

Ron just smiled and walked into the kitchen and began talking to Jan. He was not telling me what he was thinking about doing, but I guessed his plan to set Johnson up was already underway.

After talking small talk with Jan, Ron came back into the room. He started telling me his plan. He had arranged with Johnson's pimp to cut a deal with the other pimps he used to make sure that Johnson was on the rotation during the month of June. He selected June because it was after the filings had closed for District Attorney for the August primary election. Ron's plan was to have an anonymous tip given to the vice squad through Meat that told of a prostitution ring operating at the hotel where Johnson was staying. One of the prostitutes was pressured to operate a sting to catch the pimp. What they did not know was that vice was going to be an unwilling accomplice in setting Johnson up. Johnson's modus operandi was to get a room in a hotel, then call a pimp and tell him what he wanted. He had no personal contact with the pimp. The woman, women or sometimes women and men would then come up to his room and perform.

The sting for Johnson was scheduled to go off on the 17th of June, a Tuesday evening. Ron called Meat, giving him the time and place. An anonymous tip call was then made to the Petersville Gazette, the liberal daily newspaper, alerting them that a major political figure was going to get caught propositioning a prostitute that evening. The plan was to make sure that once the police found out whom they were arresting, they would not have the time or opportunity to squash the incident.

At exactly 12:30am on June 18, 1969, Harry Johnson was escorted out of the Sheraton Hotel in handcuffs. A photographer and reporter from the Gazette was standing in the hall as he came out. Before he could throw his hands up, a camera flash went off.

The reporter started asking the startled police officer a barrage of questions.

"How did you find out which room Mr. Johnson was staying in? What will he be charged with? Will his own attorneys be required to arraign him?"

The arresting officer had a puzzled look on her face. She did not know who the suspect was. As she approached the elevator, she turned her head and got the first good look at her suspect. All the muscles in her face froze.

After staring at Johnson for about 10 seconds, she started to talk. "Are you THE Harry Johnson, the District Attorney?" she asked, as the photographer camera kept clicking trying to capture the essence of her reaction.

In a very muted tone Johnson whispered, "Yes."

The police officer started sweating profusely. She also began yelling at the photographer and the reporter, telling them to leave the hotel. She rushed the DA into the elevator and blocked the door to not let the photographer and reporter in. They both ran to the exit stairs and started rushing down the steps. They were on the 10th floor and were breathless when they got to the lobby. In the lobby the arresting officer met up with her partner who immediately recognized Johnson and told his partner to take the handcuffs off. They both immediately rushed Johnson out of the hotel to their patrol car. The reporter and photographer were right behind them in pursuit. Just as they were about to get in the car, Johnson whispered in the male policeman's ear.

He then walked back to the cameraman and told him to give him the pictures he had just taken.

"These photographs are possible evidence in a criminal investigation," the policeman told the photographer as he reached to grab the camera.

"You must not have heard of the first amendment," the photographer said, pulling the camera away from his reach.

"You are in enough trouble, you don't want any more!" the reporter yelled at Johnson.

The policeman looked back and Johnson to see how far he wanted him to go. Heeding the reporter's warning, Johnson raised his hand waving the policeman off. The policeman walked back to the car and he and his partner got in with Johnson and drove off.

The reporter and the photographer went back into the hotel to use the telephone. A small crowd of hotel employees had gathered to watch. One of them yelled at the reporter as he went to use the phone.

"Was that Harry Johnson in handcuffs?"

"Yes sir," he yelled back.

I was sitting in my office waiting to hear the blow by blow when the call came in. Ron had been parked on the parking lot of the Sheraton and saw Johnson being hauled out in handcuffs. After seeing the police car pull off with Johnson in it, he drove to the nearest phone booth and called me.

"They got him. He is dead meat!" Ron yelled through the phone.

"Did anyone from the Gazette show up?" I asked.

"Yep, and they got some good pictures too. They are going to have a field day with this story. Plus, the Gazette editors have been strong opponents of Johnson. Ironically one of the reasons I opposed him was his overzealous campaign against homosexuals and prostitution. Some of the homosexuals he had personally prosecuted were employees of the Gazette. This is a story of major proportions for more than just the politics.

104

The headlines and pictures sent tremors through the body politic of Petersville. It was sweet revenge for the managing editor of the Gazette. His son was one of the homosexuals whom Johnson had prosecuted vigorously for lewd behavior. His whole career began to unravel right in front of him. The tough guy, give-no-quarter prosecutor image he had perpetuated was gone when he was arrested like a common John trying to buy some luck. The police chief, who was a friend of Johnson's, initially, tried to say it did not happen. But when he was confronted with the photos, he had to release the police report.

Within thirty days after the arrest, Johnson's life fell completely apart. The Gazette started an expose on his life and reported stories of prostitutes who claimed that Johnson traded sex with them for the promise of not being prosecuted. His wife left him and a group of lawyers filed an ethics complaint against him. And last, but not least, the police had started a criminal investigation against him. This was the straw that broke his back. On July 24th, Johnson announced he was not going to stand for re-election.

Ron's prediction had come true. Because no one else filed, Ron ended up being the only democrat of the ballot for election as District Attorney. The white boys went crazy. The Republican Central Committee filed a lawsuit. The lawsuit claimed that since the incumbent had withdrawn, the board of election commissioners was required to reopen the filing for five days to allow potential candidates to file. The Democratic Central Committee entered the case as a friend of the court citing that the same precedent should also apply to potential democratic candidates. The case was heard by a Republican judge from a rural part of the state who ruled that although it may have been local custom, it was not law.

Although we had overcome a major hurdle in winning the DA's office, the white boys who ran the city were not going to let

105

us have it without fight. A group of democratic and republican committee people had met and formed a group called the Northside Independents Association for Good Government (NIA). They said the reason they organized was to make sure that the people had a choice. Hank Popich was the spokesperson for the NIA, which meant that the downtown Civic Partners were also involved. They used a quirk in the law that allowed an independent candidate to file in the General Election. The independent candidate had to have a petition signed by at least 200 registered voters in every ward to become a qualified candidate. With the money the Civic Partners had, it was easy for them to hire people to collect the signatures. The NIA recruited a white lawyer who had been Johnson's deputy DA as their candidate. White registered voters still outnumbered blacks in Petersville, so it looked like the white democrats had found a way to thwart Ron's plan.

But alas, Ron was not giving in so easily. He used the newspaper and placed ads on the leading black oriented radio station and organized a rally to discuss the actions of the NIA at St. Marks AME church. This was an issue that had incited the ire of the entire black community. Because it was such an unusual action, it had also attracted the attention of the national press. CBS and NBC had contacted Ron for an interview and to find out when and where the rally was being held. Rita had contacted all the black elected officials and invited them to a closed-door breakfast meeting at her house at 6am on the same day of the rally. The rally was scheduled for 10am.

Although most, but not all, of the black elected officials attending the meeting would have supported Harry Johnson and were pissed off at Ron for causing this crisis, the attention that it was getting kept them from skipping the rally. They all believed that Ron was going to lose and that the white boys were doing them a favor by getting Ron out of their hair. Rita started the meeting by assailing the actions of her white democratic counterparts.

"We have all worked and delivered to the city, state, and National Democratic Party black voters in mass for many years. The Democrats never would have been able to organize an urban coalition without black voter support. My brother and his contemporaries led an exodus of black voters from the Republican Party and in 1932, which delivered the State House and the White House to the democrats, this is how we get paid? They have taken for granted that blacks vote democratic." Before she could finish her statement, the 10th ward Committeeman, Oscar Williams, interrupted her.

"Spare us the civil rights 'somebody's done somebody's wrong song.' Your boy Jackson jumped out here to run for DA without talking to anyone. There was no way he was going to beat Harry Johnson. You know it, he knows it, and everybody in this room knows it."

He walked towards the kitchen door, "I am going to get me something to eat; got to get to the rally and watch the white folks whip his ass."

The laughter from the other elected officials was long and hard. I looked over and even saw Ron laughing. Rita was pissed.

"You can leave right now if that is how you feel. White folks ain't got to ask you to bend over, your back is already bent," Rita said as she put her hands on her hips and shook in a rhythmic fashion to emphasize her point. Before Oscar could respond, Ron got up.

"Everything Oscar says is right," Ron said, winking at Rita.

"Johnson would have kicked my ass good if he had not got caught with one of the three most dangerous things a politician can get caught with: a live boy, a dead girl or a publicly traded girl."

"And even with all that, you are still going to lose. These white boys ain't going to let no nigger be the police in this town, no way no how," a voice yelled from the rear.

"You are absolutely right. White people did not and have not given up anything. It is going to be taken from them. Why don't you go ahead and feed your face while I explain how you and the others in this room are going to become major players, in spite of yourselves."

"I ain't got to listen to this shit," a voice from the rear of the room rang out.

"I am going to do this with you or without you. You can be at the front leading the crowd or on the ground being trampled."

The room got quiet. For the first time, these guys saw Ron was serious. "As usual, racism has let our colleagues from the Northend overplay their hand. Billy is now passing out a letter I have sent to the state democratic party, the National Democratic Party and every Democratic Governor, Senator and Congressman in the U.S. What these NIA boys did not take into consideration was that I was not the only democrat on the ballot in November. The Governor, Lt. Governor, all of our US Congressmen, a U.S. Senator, all the members of the State House of Representatives and half of the State Senate are up for re-election in November. I have asked the State and National Democratic Party to provide me with all the resources any other democratic candidate would receive. The initial response has been almost overwhelming. The State and National Democratic Party has sent out letters to all the Democratic elected officials who are listed as members or supporters of the NIA indicating that they will be censured if they continue to support the NIA. As of 12am this morning, I had received calls from ten white city democratic elected officials, including the Mayor, pledging their support for me."

The room had gotten quieter as I passed out additional letters and telegrams of support from the other elected officials. Ron pressed on as the mouths of the black elected officials dropped in amazement.

"The Mayor and the Governor have sent out letters to all the city democrats telling them that the two of them are going to attend the rally to show their support for me and asking them to attend. The telephone at the campaign office has been ringing off the hook with commitments from black elected officials all over the country pledging their support to me and offering to come to Petersville to help me campaign. Ladies and Gentlemen, this ain't no ordinary election no more."

Ron stopped talking and the room stayed silent for a moment. Then from the rear came a single hand clapping. It was Oscar smiling and walking up to the room to embrace Ron. Spontaneously, the rest of the crowd joined in. Ron picked up a fork and started hitting on a glass to get their attention again.

"What I did not mention to you is that I told the Mayor and the Governor the we need to negotiate a new arrangement with the Party. We are the most loyal democrats in the party, but we enjoy the least amount of the spoils," Ron added.

"He is a natural. I've never seen anything like this before. He took these hungry dogs and turned them into lambs," Rita whispered to me. "These eggs are not going to stay warm forever. We have got a lot of work to do before the rally, so eat up."

Ron wanted to leave, but I convinced him to stay and eat. I knew that he had a low opinion of these guys but I told him that he needed to become more tolerant, or at least give them the impression that he liked them. The feeling was mutual with them about us. They believed that we felt superior to them because we had been to college. I convinced Ron (for at least that morning) that he had to take the lead in developing a better working relationship with the other black elected officials.

After breakfast, Oscar suggested that we all walk into the church together as a sign of unity. I winked at Ron as he agreed with Oscar. He could now see my point. If he had initiated the request that they walk in together it would have evoked another half an hour of conversation. Since it came from Oscar, the others agreed without comment. St. Marks was only a block away from Rita's house so Ron and most of the others decided to walk.

People were walking on the sidewalks and in the streets. The streets were blocked with cars. When we got to sidewalk, I saw my mother and father walking together to the church. As my parents got closer to us, I leaned over and whispered in Ron's ear.

"That is the proof of the pudding to support your theory that the white folks overplayed their hand. My old man never even went to PTA meetings, but he is out here. Incitement works much better than excitement." I hugged my mother and father and walked with them.

When we got to the church there was a large overflow crowd standing outside waiting to get in. Janice was waiting at the door for us. She told us that all the non-reserved seats in the church were occupied and there was a limited amount of standing-room-only seats left.

Oscar was busy lining everyone up. Some white elected officials had also showed up and were going to walk in with Ron. The media was eating it up. What had started out as a protest rally had turned into a referendum on the Democratic Party. The police department had been told by the Mayor to assist traffic control. Ron had decided to try to wait on the Mayor and Governor to arrive before entering. They arrived together at 9:50am. Ron greeted the Governor warmly but was only politely cordial with the Mayor. We both suspected that he had been a behind the scenes organizer of the NIA.

As we made our entrance into St. Marks, I felt a napkin being rubbed across my face. Janice was wiping the warm tears from my face. I was overcome with the emotion of the event. St. Marks had a seating capacity of 1500 people and all the seats in the church were occupied. People were standing in the aisles two deep. A section in front of the church had been reserved for the elected officials. Only ordained ministers were allowed in the pulpit at St. Marks. As we sat down, Ron leaned over and whispered, "This is only the beginning."

The Mayor and the Governor made a speech pledging their support for Ron and denouncing the NIA. The Governor was in a tight race for re-election and did not need any defections. He urged everyone to vote straight democratic in November. The Mayor's speech was less enthusiastic. I think he could see the same thing that everyone else saw; Ron was the recipient of a lot publicity that translated into name recognition, which translated into votes. The Governor also pledged to raise money for Ron and presented a ten-thousand-dollar check to Ron at the rally.

Ron had successfully out-maneuvered the white democrats and, in the process, made himself the leading black elected official in the state. The election in November was a landslide. The NIA candidate never picked up steam. By the time the election rolled around, most of his supporters, except for a few diehards, had defected back to the fold and formally endorsed Ron. Ron was sworn in as District Attorney on January 1, 1969.

Janice and I decided to elope and got married on the same day. We stayed in town long enough to see Ron sworn in before we left to honeymoon in Jamaica.

CHAPTER 12

Exactly one month after Ron was sworn in as district attorney, he scheduled a press conference to make an announcement: my appointment as his first deputy district attorney. He also requested the resignations of all employees in the office.

The press conference was held in the courthouse in a hallway outside the courtrooms. This was 1970, and the Petersville media outlets had not adjusted to the fact that the city of Petersville had a black D.A. Some were openly hostile in their questioning of Ron. His reform move was going to disturb a lot of long-standing relationships between the staff and some reporters. The attorneys and staff were the source for stories. Ron was making the reporters' jobs more difficult and uncertain. Minutes before the conference began, I walked up to Rita, whom Ron had invited to attend.

I whispered in her ear, "This is a bold move."

"I'm just here to support my committeeman," she answered.

Ron began by reading a statement that was essentially a reprint of excerpts from his inaugural speech. After he finished, he opened the session to questions. The first came from a Gazette reporter.

"A lot of people are saying that this is just your attempt to punish the elected officials who didn't support you — especially those who were part of the NIA. How do you answer that?"

"That is not true," Ron said. "Next question, please."

The reporter was persistent. "Then your answer is 'no'? Is that what you're saying?"

"As clear as I can state it," Ron replied. "No!"

"What about those who say you are clearing house to hire your friends and to hire more black people in the office?"

"I stated very clearly — in my inaugural speech *and* in the statement I issued today — all the reasons why I am doing what I'm doing," Ron said. "I decided to run for the district attorney's office because I thought a change was needed. Change is always hard to accept, but it is inevitable. And yes, I am going to hire some of my qualified friends who also happen to be black. I am certainly not going to hire my enemies."

"How do the Democratic officials feel about this move?" one of the television reporters asked.

"You mean, how does the Democratic Committee feel? I suspect they aren't very happy."

The remainder of the press conference consisted of redundant questions by reporters who were determined to upset Ron. Nevertheless, he handled the press as if he had been doing it all his life.

***

The next morning the headline in the Gazette was positive: *"New D.A. Cleans House."*

The theme song for Ron's protractors could have been Marvin Gaye's hit song, "What's Going On?" And the hits just kept on coming.

During his first 6 months in office, Ron initiated two new units: The Sex Crimes Unit and the Organized Crime Task Force. The task force put a lot of pressure on the Syrians, who already were under the constant surveillance of the Federal Bureau of Investigations. The Syrian American Society and the Italian American Association both loudly complained to the media that they were being unfairly targeted by the new district attorney.

The hiring and rehiring of staff came off much easier than was expected. The district attorney's office was swamped with resumes from all over the metropolitan area. There were even some from outside of the city and state. It was rough going in those first 6 months. Ron was putting in long days, 7 days a week. He decided to rehire about half of the office's former employees to maintain some type of continuity.

Meanwhile, the Syrians did not sit idly as Ron tried to dismantle their power base. They responded by propping up Bumstead, Ron's old nemesis, as his challenger in the black community. In the fall of 1970, the Petersville township assessor died. The assessor ran one of the largest patronage offices in the city. Whenever there was a vacancy in such a citywide office, the Mayor had to appoint a replacement. Bumstead was able to convince the white Democrats and the Syrians to have the Mayor to appoint him assessor. The Syrians now had a man who would be a strong political rival for Ron on the Southend.

Bumstead became the perfect patsy for the Syrians and the other white democrats. He hired a Syrian as his deputy assessor — who was put there to watch him and tell him what to do. The Syrians and other white Democrats had an effective strategy:

They would have the niggers fighting each other, keeping them too blind, too divided to build a base strong enough to challenge the whites.

Of the five black wards, Bumstead and the Syrians controlled three of them. After the election Ron formed a coalition with Oscar Williams, which gave him influence over the other two wards. Bumstead made it clear to the press and others that he was going to support another candidate against Ron when he ran for re-election in 1974. Except for Williams, Ron had not cultivated any political relationships among the black committee people.

Near the end of 1970, Ron set up a meeting with Williams, Rita and me to discuss the "Syrian problem."

The meeting was scheduled to be held at Williams' real-estate office on a Tuesday after work. The office was on Madison Street, a main thoroughfare in the Southend that was home to a lot of dry-goods stores and other commerce. In route to the meeting with Oscar, Ron was stopping at Ming's Onions to get some Chinese food. That was not the real name of the place, but George had given it that name in high school because of the uneven onions-to-meat ratio that came with each dish.

Rita and I arrived early and were sitting in Williams' office making small-talk with Williams when Ron drove up with Meat. Williams' real estate office was in a store front with a large plate glass window on the front that had the words Oscars Williams Real Estate Management and Sales.

"I don't know why we got here so early," I said as I got up and walked over to a small table that had a coffee pot and cups set up for the meeting. "Ron is always late."

Rita and Oscar chuckled and nodded their heads in agreement. I was picking up the coffee pot when through the window, I saw Ron's black Buick pull up. Ron got out of the car and was opening the back door to get the food when I saw the glass from the window in his car breaking. At the same instant, Ron and Meat instinctively fell to the ground. I pushed Rita to the floor and yelled at Williams to get his ass down. He had already grabbed a gun from his desk drawer and was walking toward the front door. A bullet crashed through the large plate-glass window splitting Williams' head open. Rita screamed. I crawled to the side of the desk and grabbed the phone to call the police. Breathlessly, I reported the district attorney, his police driver and Williams had been shot. Then I crawled back to Rita to calm her. She was badly shaken. I called out to Williams to see if he was conscious. He did not respond. I checked his vital signs but could not get a pulse.

I could hear sirens approaching and saw a police unit come to a screeching stop next to Ron's car. Ron was able to get his wallet out to show his identification to the ambulance driver.

"My driver is bleeding badly. You need to move him out of here fast!" Ron yelled at the ambulance attendant.

"You don't look so good yourself sir. It looks like you have been wounded also," the ambulance driver responded.

"Don't worry about me, it is just a flesh wound. Meat has a stomach wound. He needs attention immediately."

"Just lie still, Mister," an ambulance driver said. "The police have got to secure the area to make sure that whoever was shooting at you has stopped, before we can move you. Use your belt to make a tourniquet. I'll try to get over to you."

Police cars surrounded the scene. Several policemen reached Ron and were using their bodies to shield him as they moved him away from the car.

"Is anybody in here?" yelled a voice from the rear of the office.

"Yes, there are three of us in here. A man has been shot. He needs help right away," I hollered back.

Two policemen had come through the back door of Oscar's building. They stood near the office door where we were sitting. One of them crawled to Williams and checked his vital signs.

"This one is dead!" he shouted to his partner. He, in turn, instructed us. "Crawl slowly back this way to the rear door."

Rita and I crawled out the back door and breathed deeply to keep from hyperventilating. Rita was still crying. I identified myself to one of the policemen and asked him to take Rita and me to the hospital. He said we had to wait until the homicide unit arrived because we were witnesses to a murder.

I went back inside to call Janice and tell her what had happened. She was extremely upset and wanted to leave work to be with me. I told her instead to call Ron and Meat's parents and to go to the hospital to be with them. I assured her I was fine and would come straight to the hospital as soon as I was finished with the police.

The cops questioned Rita and me for almost an hour. There was little we could tell them. Afterward, they escorted us to the hospital. Janice, who had picked up Ron's parents, was in the waiting room when Rita and I arrived. She immediately ran to me.

The scene at the hospital was a zoo. Police were everywhere, trying to make sure nothing else happened. They kept the reporters, cameramen and television crews at a safe distance from us — in front of the emergency entrance.

Ron had been shot in the arm, but the bullet had passed through the limb. Meat's wound was more serious: a bullet had gone through his shoulder and he had lost a lot of blood.

"What the hell is going on, Billy?" Ron's mother asked. "Who did this awful thing?"

"I don't know, Mrs. Jackson," I answered, even as a list of possible suspects ran through my mind. But this was not the time or place for me to express any opinions.

"It was them damn Syrians!" Ron's father exploded. "They been mad ever since Ron won and threatened to end their stronghold on the Southend!" He took a few steps to the nurses' station and began beating on the counter.

"I want to see my son or his doctor — right now! He said. "We been here an hour, and nobody will say shit!" A nurse told him to calm down and said she would go back to the treatment area to get someone to talk to him. I could see where Ron got his persistence. Less than five minutes later, a white-haired doctor emerged to talk with us.

He said Ron was doing fine, his wound had been treated and he probably would be admitted overnight for observation. Meat was still in surgery, but his prognosis was positive.

"What kind of observation does Ron need?" his mother asked.

"We want to make sure there is no internal bleeding or other complications," the doctor replied. At that moment, T.C. walked in. He asked me about Ron, and I repeated what the doctor told us.

"I'm going to spend the night here," he said. "I don't trust the police. They could be the same motherfuckers that popped Ron. How's Meat doin'?"

"He's in surgery, but they think he's going to be alright."

"This was a professional hit, Billy. Somebody hired a pro to hit Ron. I told him he was fuckin' with some powerful people when he became DA, but he didn't believe me."

A few minutes later, the doctor told us we could see Ron. He had been given some pain pills and would be awake for only a few minutes. When we reached his room, Ron was sitting up, smiling. He was either the best black actor in the world or a bullet had grazed his head, too, because he was laughing and joking when we came in. We visited for about 10 minutes, and then a nurse came in to say it was time to leave. Ron said his good-byes but asked T.C. and me to stay for a minute.

"Is Meat okay?" Ron asked. "He took a bullet for me and maybe saved my life!"

"The doctor says he's going to be alright," I said. "He's still in surgery."

"These are some strong motherfuckers," Ron shook his head. "They tried to kill me in broad daylight!"

"I'm going to stay with you through the night," T.C. said. "These are some bold and desperate motherfuckers, man. If they

119

would try to kill you in broad daylight, they might try to do it in the hospital!"

After visiting Ron, I went to check on Meat. His mother was a nervous wreck. After consoling her, I talked with the doctor. Meat was out of surgery and listed as stable. The doctor said the operation was a success, but it would be another 24 hours before he could say for certainty that Meat would make it. He was in the intensive-care unit and could only see two people at a time. I escorted his mother in to see him. Meat was resting, so I decided there was nothing else I could do at the hospital.

I thought some of Ron must have rubbed off on me because I began thinking about the exclusive story I could tell as an eyewitness to — and a victim of — the incident.

Clearly, the shooting was one of the most newsworthy stories ever to happen in Petersville. The police, still unsure who had been the target, escorted Rita and me home. An officer posted a police car overnight at Rita's house. The vision of seeing Ron and Meat shot down kept me from getting any real sleep that night. Nevertheless, I was up early the next morning, answering questions from the local and national press. As a result, I did not leave the house until after 9 am. A police car with two plain-clothes detectives was sitting outside my house. They said they were supposed to stay with me until further notice. I went to the office to brief the staff and to make sure things continued to run smoothly. I asked Janice to go to the hospital and said I'd meet her there later.

The scene at the hospital was a bigger media circus than it had been the previous night. Television crews from all the local affiliates — as well as reporters and cameramen from the NBC, CBS and ABC networks — had been camped out there since 6am.

When I got to Ron's room he was sitting up, reading the Gazette and the Herald. T.C. was still there.

"Close the door, Billy, 'cause we need to talk," Ron said, folding his paper and putting it at the foot of his bed. "This shit is hot! I've been getting calls from the New York Times, CBS, NBC and the Today Show. I need your help to prepare for a press conference I'm going to hold in about an hour."

"Okay, let me think," I said. "The first thing: it should be brief. You should express your deepest condolences for Oscar and his family. Oscar was killed trying to protect you and the others, and he will always be remembered for that. You should stress that this type of lawlessness will not be tolerated, and that it will not deter nor intimidate you. That should be it."

"I like it," Ron said. "T.C., what do you think?"

"I already think all of y'all talk too much — so the briefer, the better," he said. "The shitheads who did this want you to panic and be cautious."

"The next thing we're going to do is recruit someone to run in each black ward," Ron said. "First, for the committee seats, and then we'll go after the city council slots. I'm going to kick Bumstead and his Syrian sand niggers in the ass!"

"I'm going to tighten the screws on all the illicit shit the Syrians are doing." Ron was talking faster as he went. "Grand juries are going to look at all aspects of organized crime in Petersville. T.C., you need to tell your friends to cool out for a while. For the next two years, we are going to conduct a crusade against crime and corruption unlike anything this city has ever seen! These motherfuckers are going to be crying that shooting me was the worst thing they could ever have done! I was looking for the hammer, Billy — and they served it to me on a silver platter."

"It's your hand, man," I said. "I'll play it any way you want."

Ron was released from the hospital on Saturday, just in time to attend Williams' funeral. He played the wounded-martyr role to the hilt. He had two policemen with him now. Williams' funeral rivaled Connors' in size, in most part due to the publicity of the shooting.

CHAPTER 13

The political revolution in Petersville ran concurrently with the 1972 re-election campaign of President Richard Nixon.

The Democratic National Convention was held in Miami that year, but neither Ron nor I attended. We did, however, block Bumstead from attending by tying up the delegates in the Fifth Congressional District.

The district was allocated 6 delegates to the convention. Ron, Rita and Ennis were selected, but only Rita went. Ron had no intention of going, but he wanted to keep Bumstead from developing any momentum.

It was during the 1972 presidential campaign that the now-infamous Watergate burglary occurred. Yet the murder of George Martin and the assassination attempt on Ron seemed a more serious threat to democracy than a second-rate burglary to steal files or bug the offices of the DNC. After the shooting incident, the FBI and a lawyer from the U.S. Attorney's office interviewed Rita and me. They told us that, unless they got lucky, the chances of catching the killer were slim. I got the impression the murder of a black man was not that important.

Although Ron's term did not expire until 1973, the Syrians decided to start two years early in their efforts to defeat him.

They recruited Daniel Dwyer Jr., who came from a well-known Irish Catholic political family.

His grandfather immigrated to Petersville from Ireland with his family in 1889. Dwyer's great-grandfather and grandfather were career police officers. His great-grandfather was the first Irish Catholic to rise to the rank of commander in Petersville. The elder Dwyer was a police officer during a period of time when organized crime controlled the politics in Petersville. Employment in all segments of city government was patronage. You could not get a job with the city without a political referral.

Dwyers family settled in an area of town called the Patch which was controlled by an Irish gang called Egan's rats. His great-grandfather's father died of yellow fever two months after they arrived in Petersville. He had seven children, three boys and four girls. At thirteen, Dwyer's great-grandfather became the man of the house and had to get a job. His father was a massive man, six-foot four inches and weighed 250 pounds. He had got job as a no-show laborer working for a construction company, but his real job was an enforcer with the Egan gang. After he died Dwyer's great-grandfather went to meet with Joe Egan, the gang leader of Egan rats and also a democratic committeeman.

Egan was eager to hire Dwyer, but his real goal to recruit and groom some young smart Irishmen to become members of the Petersville police department which at the time was predominately white Anglo-Saxon Protestants (WASPS). He told young Dwyer that he wanted him to stay in school and that the gang would take care of his family. Dwyer did just that and after he graduated from high school, he joined the Petersville Police Department as one of five Irish Catholics to join. He used his connections with Irish gangsters to get on the police force and to rise through the ranks to become a captain. He spent a large part of his career as commander of the Petersville police department's organized crime unit. Dwyer's grandfather followed in his footsteps and also rose to commander, in charge of the organized crime unit.

He had eight children, four boys and four girls. All of the boys became lawyers. Daniel Dwyer Jr.'s, father served as district attorney from 1950-59.

In March 1965, the Saturday Evening Post looked at organized crime in Petersville. The article described Captain Dwyer as an organized crime "mole" on the police force and said organized crime flourished during his tenure as commander of the Organized Crime Unit (OCU). The piece linked Captain Dwyer and the now-defunct Irish organized-crime syndicates based in the Southend. When the blacks moved in, the Irish left and the Syrians filled the vacuum. The article also implied Captain Dwyer was on the Syrians' payroll for years.

The article said when his son, Daniel Dwyer Sr., was appointed district attorney in 1950 to fill a vacancy created by the death of the incumbent, the Syrians provided the support he needed for the appointment. Before the appointment, the Syrians and Egan were loudly voicing their intentions to support the governor's opposition. Immediately after Dwyer was appointed, the Syrians and Egan endorsed the governor — a year early — for re-election.

The Post article also reported Captain Dwyer acted as a negotiator, in an arrangement with the Chicago arm of La Cosa Nostra, that allowed the Syrians to reimburse the Irish for their Southend "business enterprises." The Petersville crime syndicate had been controlled by the Chicago mob since the days of Al Capone. This amicably-negotiated reimbursement set the stage for a friendship between the Dwyers and the Syrians that is still intact.

So when Dwyer Jr. announced his intention to file for district attorney, the political writers at the Petersville Gazette immediately abandoned Ron. The newspaper had been touting Ron as one of the best district attorneys in the history of the city. Suddenly, Dwyer was their choice — the "perfect" white boy.

A Harvard law graduate with a Yale undergraduate degree, Dwyer had been groomed well for the task-at-hand. The Gazette editorialized that Dwyer represented a breath of fresh air on the Petersville political scene, and he would provide a high quality of leadership as district attorney.

I immediately called Robert Klingman, managing editor of the Gazette, to ask him why the newspaper had virtually endorsed Dwyer almost a year-and-a-half before the election.

"Well, we. . .we did not endorse Dwyer," he sputtered. "The paper was just. . .just expressing an op-pinion that we. . .thought it was good, uh, that there was a high quality of people, uh, interested in public service."

I didn't let him off easily.

"That's such a bullshit answer — and you know it!" I yelled into the phone. "You can't even get your mouth to say it properly. It sounds like a left-handed way for your paper to let white people know that y'all are not in the nigger DA's back-pocket. If Dwyer was having any doubts about which way the Gazette was going to go, you certainly erased them for him!"

"Everything is not black-and-white," Klingman said in low voice, trying hard to resist reacting to my accusation. "If I offended you, I'm sorry."

"You don't have a fuckin' clue about what offends me!" I growled. "What's offensive to me is the patronizing attitude of you pseudo-liberals, who support public accommodations for blacks but only give lip-service to real power-sharing. But I'm not going to bore you with what is obviously a wasted conversation," I said. "The ass-kickin' we give to Dwyer and his

126

organized-crime associates will do our talking from now on. Goodbye, Mr. Klingman."

I slammed down the phone and began laughing, because I knew Klingman was calling in his political reporters to ask them about my statement, about Dwyer and about organized crime.

There is a saying in politics "Overnight is a lifetime" and that certainly applied to the Petersville media. Before the SIA, and its stunning victories in the 1972 primaries, Ron was the darling of the press. His attack on organized crime, his creation of a Crimes Against Women Unit and his crackdown on illegal drug-trafficking were lauded as timely and progressive.

But when Ron showed how these positive policies could be converted into political empowerment, the white boys who ran the major media outlets took notice. If the SIA continued to be successful, Petersville could elect a black man as mayor — and the media would play no part in it.

Opposition to Ron came from two camps.

One was the pseudo-liberal element, which wanted to slow him down and then choose the city's first black mayor. This group was led by Popich, a mouthpiece for the Petersville business coalition. The formation of the SIA was a threat to Popich and other Jews who had sold themselves to the Protestant-dominated, Anglo-Saxon business community as the gatekeepers of the black community.

The others — like the Dwyers and their redneck constituents from the north side — were just old-fashioned racists who could not tolerate the idea that Petersville could elect a black mayor.

Both groups merged their interests to defeat Ron and thwart the efforts of the SIA. Ron, characteristically, was unphased by what was developing.

After my conversation with Klingman, I met him for lunch at the Downtown Athletic Club. For 75 years, the DAC had been an exclusive, racist and sexist private club for white Anglo-Saxon males. Ron became a member only because a DAC bylaw made the mayor, the chief of police and the district attorney ex-officio members. Although I did not like going to the DAC for anything, Ron got a rush seeing the irritated faces of the die-hard-racist members when they saw him walk in. Since he had become a member, the DAC admitted two women and two black men. Of course, the status-quo white boys blamed Ron; it was his fault they had to change their policy and allow women and blacks to join.

We had lunch in a private room. When I told Ron of my conversation with Klingman, he remained expressionless.

"You're going to have to take my word on this: Some things are going to happen that will allow the Dwyer problem to take care of itself," he said. "I just finished meeting with the new U.S. attorney."

The new man replaced Ed Ottinger, who had incurred the wrath of a powerful Fortune 500 company's chief executive officer. Ottinger had staged a surprise search and seizure of records and other evidence at the company's corporate headquarters in downtown Petersville. As a result, Ottinger was not re-appointed by President Nixon.

"Take care of itself in what way?" I asked.

"In a legal way that won't involve me directly," Ron said. "The new U.S. attorney is going to use his office to focus on organized crime, public corruption and drug-dealing. He's particularly interested in the Syrians' crime organization and their connection with the Teamsters Union Pension Fund. Try and guess who represents the Teamsters Pension Fund."

"Danny Boy Junior?" I laughed.

"Yep!"

"Say no more. Let's eat and get out of here so I can revel in this good news!"

Klingman's response to our phone conversation was to have the Gazette do a feature story on Ron. But what was supposed to be an upbeat profile series turned out to be a six-day hatchet job.

The story traced Ron's life back through high school, his college years as member of SNCC and his current public office. It was a feeding-frenzy for Ron's enemies.

The newspaper detailed his college days' protest activities and spotlighted his record of 17 arrests. The series attempted to paint Ron as a communist sympathizer.

The Gazette tried to punch holes in the conviction rate of the district attorney's office under Ron's tenure, saying that — although the office had a higher rate of convictions — it also had fewer prosecutions.

In one interview, a Gazette reporter asked Ron why he had fewer prosecutions than his predecessor. Ron replied it was part of a quality-control system that concentrated on prosecuting the guilty as opposed to the innocent. He also cited that fact that he was not prosecuting gays under what he called as "the archaic state sodomy and sexual deviance laws." The reporter was a homosexual, so the interview ended there.

The Gazette series accused Ron of political cronyism in his hiring practices and detailed the hiring of several lawyers who had run for elective office after being hired by the district attorney's office.

Again, Ron's answer was straightforward: "Participation in civic and community activities is not only encouraged by me, but also rewarded. My theory is that good citizens make good employees. Are they forced to participate? The answer is no."

The rest of the articles had the same redundant theme.

Ron had received a lot of goodwill from the press. Now the same press that once called him "the brightest light on Petersville's political horizon" was demonizing him and thereby eroding his already-tenuous white support base.

CHAPTER 14

"Overnight can be a lifetime" proved as true of a saying about organized crime as it did about politics.

While the Syrians and their allies were putting into motion a sure-fire plan to defeat Ron and stop his budding rise to power, the long-time leader of the Petersville Mafia, Tony Di Marco was killed by a car bomb. The murder, in January 1973, created a huge gangland leadership vacuum in Petersville. Chicago crime bosses moved quickly to name Ansur Thomas as the temporary boss in Petersville. This was the first time a non-Sicilian — or even a non-Italian — became the boss of La Cosa Nostra in Petersville.

Thomas had been the head of the Syrian crime family for years and a close ally of Black Connors. He was thought to be in his mid-70s, but his real age was unknown. Thomas and most other Syrian and Lebanese Christian residents of Petersville had migrated to the United States in the late 1890's, fleeing religious persecution from Muslim-controlled Syria. There were no more than 100 Syrians living in Petersville at the time. They settled in in what was called then and now the river wards along the banks of the Mississippi. Most people who lived in river wards worked on the wharf. They were either in the hauling business or they worked as stevedores or longshoremen.

Several families had been in the drayage or hauling business in Syria and decided to do the same when they arrived in Petersville.

At that time, organized crime was led by Irish and Italian gangs who ruled the river wards. When the Syrians opened their businesses, either Italian or Irish gangsters, depending on which side of the street the business was on, demanded payment for protection, immediately confronting them. Initially, the Syrians balked, but after several of their businesses were either destroyed or severely damaged, they decided to form their own gang. This was the first time Captain Dwyer and Ansur Thomas met. Thomas led a Syrian gang that was stealing commodities from barges on the wharf. One of the Syrian families was in the hauling business and had 10 horse-drawn wagons used to unload barges in the daytime. At night, Thomas and his gang used the same horses to steal from the same barges.

The Post article said that Captain Dwyer caught them one night and established a profitable turn-your-head-the-wrong-way arrangement. Over the years, the enterprise grew to become one of the largest transportation and hauling businesses in the Midwest.

Over time the Syrians transformed a number of their illicit activities into legitimate businesses. There had been nothing reported recently in the press to suggest the organized crime families were upset enough at each other to let their dispute erupt so violently in the public. So I wondered…was this what Ron was talking about?

If Ron was feeling any stress from the pressure of the campaign to defeat him, he didn't show it. In fact, it was during that time Ron introduced his friends to Lyzette Stanford. Lyzette was a model, originally from Jamaica, who lived in New York City. Ron met Lyzette while visiting Wiley in New York. He was immediately smitten by her. After several trips that he had disguised as business trips, Ron invited Lyzette to Petersville and asked Janice to host a dinner party for her. Janice convinced a Jamaican friend to prepare a native feast.

The dinner was held three weeks after the DiMarco killing. I had not been able to talk to Ron about it, and I was sure the news reports did not accurately report the full story. Lyzette was visiting for the weekend, so Janice invited her and Ron to dinner at our house. Although Janice always bubbled over with Southern hospitality, this was not just an ordinary invitation to dinner.

Dinner was scheduled for 7pm, but Ron and Lyzette arrived an hour early. I told Ron I wanted to talk to him about the DiMarco murder, and I knew Janice wanted to give Lyzette the third-degree. We didn't know what to expect, but when we saw Lyzette getting out of Ron's car, her stunning looks almost put the two of us into a catatonic trance. I had seen a lot of women in my lifetime, but Lyzette was the most beautiful I had ever seen. Her body looked as if someone had poured it into this black-silk, half-mini skirt. Her shoulder-length hair had a silky black texture that almost matched her complexion. As I opened the door to let them in, Ron was quick to let me know he was aware he had sufficiently shocked both of us.

"Close your mouth, Billy!" Ron whispered. "I know just how you feel because I felt the same way when I first saw Lyzette. Ain't she the most beautiful woman you ever seen? And her looks are only the icing on the cake," Ron said with an expression like a cat who had just caught the fattest mouse in the world.

Janice elbowed me and reached out her hand to greet Lyzette. "Hi, I'm Janice Strayhorn. Welcome to our home and to Petersville. This mummy standing next to me is my husband, Billy."

"I'm so glad that I am finally getting to meet you," Lyzette said with a pronounced, charming and very-British accent. "Ron is the first man I have dated who was more concerned about me meeting a woman who was not his mother. And this must be Billy! It is a pleasure to meet you, also. Ron has told me so much about you."

"I am only half as bad as he described," I said, moving a part of my body for the first time since I saw her.

"Oh, quite the contrary, Ron credits you with all he has been able to accomplish," she said.

"Ron told us you were Jamaican, but you have a decidedly-British accent," I said, handing her a glass of wine.

"I was born in Jamaica. My parents sent me to school in England. I often call myself an Asian Rastafarian. My father is a native Jamaican. My mother is of Chinese descent. It is not well known, but a number of Chinese settled in Jamaica during the early part of the 20th Century," Lyzette said.

Chinese were brought to Jamaica to allegedly replace slavery, which had been officially outlawed in the British Empire. They were subjected to another form of indentured servitude which was the same or *worse* than slavery.

Suddenly she asked Janice, "Are those ox-tails you are cooking, girl?" It came out in a blend of broken-English and Jamaican dialect.

"Yes, those are ox-tails but no, I am not cooking them," Janice said. "I know Ron and Billy want to talk, so let me introduce you to the cook." She ushered Lyzette to the kitchen.

As they left, I lifted my glass in Ron's direction. "You done good, boy! You done real good!"

"Agreed! I think I am in love, Billy," Ron beamed as our glasses met to complete the toast. "Lyzette is one of the most beautiful — and most intelligent — people I have ever met."

"I do want to talk to you about her some more, but my curiosity is killing me about what the real story is behind the DiMarco killing," I said, motioning Ron to sit on the couch.

"It all started over who was going to control the city towing contracts," Ron began. "DiMarco's family has had a contract to provide towing for the city for the past 30 years. No matter who was mayor, it was understood that the contract for towing belonged to them. The city contract gave them a legitimate front for what essentially served as a chop shop for a national car-theft ring. The FBI came to me six months ago to let me know they were investigating the DiMarco towing business," Ron said. "They secured court-orders for telephone and wire taps and they bugged every known place that DiMarco frequented. The first two months of surveillance didn't reveal much."

"Then last November, a telephone call between DiMarco and Martie Sayles was intercepted. Sayles is a distant relative of Ansur Thomas. His family has always been characterized as the black sheep of the Syrian clan. Well, the FBI got Sayles on tape — screaming at DiMarco, telling him he double-crossed him on the towing contract. Martie said the new towing contract that went into effect the first day of January was supposed to be split equally between the two of them. DiMarco said he changed his mind and was going to give Sayles only 30 percent. Martie was pissed, and after they finished calling each other every derogatory name in the book, Martie told DiMarco he was not going to let him fuck him out of what's coming to him. That was all that was heard about that — until the middle of December, when DiMarco got a call from Ansur Thomas, who was trying to mediate the feud between DiMarco and Sayles. DiMarco told Thomas he was not giving 'that sand-nigger nothing now.' He said he was doing him a favor and he might reconsider if Sayles apologized."

"Ansur told DiMarco not to do anything until he heard from him. Well, the next thing we knew, a car explosion killed DiMarco." Ron got up and poured himself another glass of wine.

"That's a strong move for Sayles," I said. "I always figured him some sort of Damon Runyan character — a lot of talk but no heart. What do you think is going to happen next?"

"The Feds decided to tap Sayles's phone and tow-lot office. They learned he and some of the younger members of the Syrian family are not happy with the selection of Ansur Thomas as boss. These younger members didn't know who Ansur was — and they didn't care. They think he's old and soft. They were feeling a tremendous amount of heat from the organized-crime bureau that I set up. They thought Ansur could use his political connections to have the heat turned down if he wanted to — but he refused to do it," Ron went on.

"Ansur told them he was not going to use up his chips to help people who were into drug-trafficking. Martie asked Ansur to give him the city towing contracts, but Ansur said he had to get permission from the Chicago people."

"The Feds think Martie is on drugs or something," Ron said. "He was overhead setting up what they think was a hit on Ansur. They took the tape to Ansur and tried to cut a deal with him, but he told them to go fuck themselves. He would rather die than snitch. I told the Feds I wasn't going to do anything unless Ansur filed a complaint. So right now, we are just waiting to see who will make the first move — and hopefully, we will be there to lock all of 'em up!"

"Dinner is ready, fellas," a feminine voice called. "The meeting is over. You've got to pay attention to your women now!"

136

It was Janice calling from the dining room. "Lyzette and I have had a wonderful talk. Now I know all I need to know to recommend you need to pay some attention to her, Ron."

"I fully intend to," Ron answered as he squeezed Lyzette's hand and walked to the table. As he pulled her chair out, the doorbell rang. I looked through the door's window. It was Meat.

"Damn, Meat," I said. "I'm sorry. If I knew you were out there, I would have invited you in."

"I know that, but I had to stay in the car to listen to the radio," he said. "There was a report came across that I thought you might want to know about," Meat said as he walked over to Ron. He leaned over and whispered in his ear. Ron's head turned completely around.

"Are you sure?"

"Positively!" Meat said. "I called University Hospital to check and they confirmed it."

"Ansur Thomas was gunned down as he left Mass this afternoon. It looks like the war has begun. I'll be busy tomorrow. But that's not going to spoil my enjoyment of this meal and of the company. Let's eat!"

I looked at Ron and said, "You can't say this, Ron, but I will. I hope the bastards commit fratricide for all the grief they've caused our community over the years. As Malcolm said, 'It is just all the chickens coming home to roost.'"

The next day's headline was blunt: HEAD OF SYRIAN MOB SLAIN IN GANGLAND-STYLE EXECUTION.

Two days later, three members of Sayles' gang were shot down when coming out of a restaurant. A week later, a bomb exploded in Sayles' brother's garage. It did not kill him but left him paralyzed from the waist down.

137

Ron and the U.S. attorney held a joint press conference and pledged to work together to prosecute the people responsible for the murders.

Martie Sayles went underground. The Syrians employed by the city government did not report for work after a grandson of Ansur Thomas was shot to death on the Petersville City Hall parking lot.

The gang war had gotten out of hand. A task force — including elements of the FBI, the State Patrol, Petersville Police, the district attorney's office and U.S. attorney's office — obtained search warrants and raided the Sayles towing company offices. Lawmen found hundreds of weapons — along with a file that listed the vehicle identification numbers of *thousands* of stolen cars that had been "processed" at the towing lot.

The press had a field day with the story.

A warrant was issued for Sayles' arrest, but he was able to elude the authorities for two months before he was found slumped over in a car in Miami with a bullet in his head. It looked like a professional hit. Ron surmised the Chicago mob wanted Martie dead. They figured this might reduce the heat on them.

Fifteen people were killed in the gang war, decimating the leadership ranks in both warring Syrian factions. The impact on the Syrians' political base was even more devastating. The Gazette dedicated an entire front page to the story of the gang war and the history of the Syrians' involvement in politics and organized crime in Petersville. Using some of the research by the Saturday Evening Post, the Gazette updated the story by including the names of politicians from the mayor to the governor who were either controlled by the Syrians or who were suspected of being in their sphere of influence.

The Gazette story traced the history of Syrian involvement in politics and corruption in Petersville from the late 1920s to the present.

Many people who ordinarily would have been afraid to talk openly about the Syrians were very forthcoming; understandable in view of the virtual destruction of the Syrian organization following the rash of murders, investigations and recent prosecutions.

The Syrians were able to do to themselves what police and other law-enforcement authorities were unable or — in some cases — unwilling to accomplish in the past 30 years.

It was amazing how clearly the paper trail showed the connections and how it detailed the relationships between the Syrians and prominent elected and appointed officials in Petersville and the state.

CHAPTER 15

Almost two months before the opening day for filing for election, members of the Dwyer campaign staff began camping out in front of the Petersville Board of Election Commissioners building.

Dwyer wanted to ensure his would be the first name listed on the ballot for district attorney. Because it was two days after Thanksgiving and usually a slow news day, Dwyer was able to get good coverage from the print and electronic media outlets.

Ron had planned to do the same thing, but Dwyer had beat him to it. He had planned to put his people there that coming Monday morning, but he was a little late. He had rented a bus that had been converted into a luxury motorhome and hired a crew of "volunteers." Undaunted, Ron put plan B into play. At the same time, he was telling the press that being first on the ballot was not too important, he set in motion a plan to take Dwyer's spot.

The Board of Election Commissioners did not monitor or sanction the candidates or their representatives who were waiting in line for a position on the ballot. The filing order was strictly on a first-come, first-served basis: When the first filing day arrived, whomever was first in line to file got his name first on the ballot.

Ron sent his crew to the election board on Monday morning. They rented a parking space for the recreational vehicle on a lot next to the election board building. Ron hired 12 volunteers to work three 8-hour shifts in teams of four. Dwyer had two-man teams working two 12-hour shifts. Ron told his crew to get friendly with Dwyer's people by offering them coffee and food and by letting them warm up in the R.V. He was laying the groundwork for a double-cross.

On New Year's Eve, Petersville got 10 inches of snow which made sitting in line outside in the cold and snow a serious challenge.

At About 6pm Ron came down to visit his volunteers. He brought with him boxes of food and liquor for a New Year's Eve party his volunteers had planned. Ron told his volunteers to make sure that they invited Dwyer's workers to the party. When Dwyer's workers found out that Ron was throwing a party for his workers, they got visibly upset. One of Dwyer's volunteers was so angry he told one of Ron's crew he would help get Dwyer's spot for a fee. The Dwyer defector agreed to desert his post when his partner broke for lunch and he would not return. This would allow Ron's crew to grab the vacant seat and claim it for Ron.

The unofficial rule was: If you move, you lose.

Ron had his people take photographs of the vacant seat. Then he called the press and the elections director to say Dwyer's crew had abandoned the seat.

After the other Dwyer team member finished his lunch break and returned, he was furious. He tried to physically remove Ron's man from the chair but decided he was outmatched. He left to call Dwyer.

But Dwyer, who was attending a New Year's Eve party and didn't get home until 3am, could not be reached.

In fact, Dwyer didn't find out about the incident until he read it in the morning paper. He protested to the election board but was told the board had no jurisdiction over what happened outside the building.

The press loved it. The headline in the Gazette read: "Musical Chairs at Board of Elections."

***

It was January 1973, and the Watergate hearing was in the newspapers, on the radio, on television and was becoming part of everyone's conversations. Most of the antics Nixon's campaign staffers did were mild compared to what I saw in my hometown.

Once, Ron used several attractive female college students to infiltrate the campaign of a candidate who Hank Popich filed to run for Congress against Ennis. I was with Ron one evening at the Living Room Lounge when one of these Mata Hara's came by to see him. We were having a drink at the bar when a dark, petite sister came up to Ron.

"Mr. Jackson, I need to talk to you," she whispered in his ear. Ron's eyes got as big as late-season watermelons as he turned around to get a better look at her.

"Let's go to that booth and talk," he said, as he grabbed her arm. "Get the drinks and bring them over to the table," Ron gestured waving his hand at me.

My mind was racing a mile-a-minute, trying to figure out who and what she was.

"I'm sorry," Ron said to the young lady. "Do you want anything to drink?"

"I'll have a Coke."

As she slid her tight, sensuous body across the red leather seat, I was reminded of the old saying: "Youth is wasted on the

142

young." I went to the bar, ordered her a coke and returned with our drinks.

"What's so important that you had to come down here to tell me?" Ron asked, his eyebrows arching to accentuate his discomfort. "I thought we had developed a system for you to use to contact me."

"You told me to contact you immediately if I heard certain names being mentioned in any conversation at the campaign headquarters," she said. "This afternoon, I overheard Mr. Bates mention that James Turner had committed to him his support for Dwyer." Turner was a Democratic committeeman and State Representative from the Southend.

"That lying, double-crossing motherfucker!" Ron growled. "I already gave that punk more than two grand. Well, I knew that son of a bitch was not to be trusted. But I've got something for him: I'm going to have James Ford file for Committeeman! Beating him will be a breeze especially since it is common knowledge that he lives and has lived in Los Angeles for the past 5 years," Ron said. "I've kept the wolves off his ass long enough. Were any other names mentioned?"

"None that were on your list."

"Thank you very much," Ron said. "You done good, girl. You need to leave before somebody from Bates' camp sees you talking to me."

"They all went to a fundraiser," the little vixen said as she slipped out of the seat. "But I do understand what you mean. I'll call you at the regular time Saturday." Her body swayed just enough to make everyone in the place who was not blind turn and look as she sashayed out the door.

"Will I have to start calling you Pimpin' Ronnie now? What the fuck was that all about?" I said sarcastically.

"That is my information network," Ron said. "Don't ask for a more detailed explanation. That way, you can maintain the ability to deny and say honestly you don't know."

"Have you planted these information bimbos in all the enemy camps?" I asked.

"I prefer to describe them as converts who I was able to turn around to my way of thinking by making them a better offer to work for me. I've developed a very effective information network, if I do say so myself."

"Doesn't it bother you that you're invading a person's privacy by spying on them? You're using the same tactics we accuse our enemies of using."

"Yes, and I would not have done it any other way," Ron said. "I can't use African politics or Zulu politics to win in Petersville. It's the white Anglo-Saxon politicians who taught me how to win."

"It sounds sleazy, like a smaller version of the shit that got Richard Nixon in trouble."

"I don't have a problem with what Nixon is accused of doing," Ron said. "He is the president of the most-powerful nation in the world. Here is a man empowered to drop hundreds of tons of bombs on Hanoi but cannot hide a minor burglary. Politics is not tiddlywinks. It is civilized warfare, and you have to soak your face in rock salt to get a skin tough enough to survive."

This conversation about doing the right thing came too late for Ron. He had entered politics at a time when the political paradigm was "All's fair in politics and war" and he had proven himself to be a worthy soldier.

***

Humiliated, from losing his space in line, Dwyer retreated into three months of silence. This perfectly suited Ron because it gave him time to get married. He and Lyzette had decided to get married in her home country of Jamaica. More than 100 of Ron's closest friends and family flew to Jamaica to attend his wedding.

It was a good thing the event was scheduled for a Sunday, because the male members of the wedding party got so wasted at the Ron's bachelor party that Friday that they missed the Saturday-afternoon rehearsal.

The wedding went off without a hitch. Ron and Lyzette honeymooned in the Seychelles, an island-nation on the west coast of Africa. On the way back home from Jamaica, Jan and I decided to stop in Rio de Janeiro for a second honeymoon. When we got back to Petersville, we learned that Ebony magazine had run a three-page pictorial on the wedding. The article called it "the wedding against which all others should be judged." The affair cost Lyzette's family more than $30,000.

I told Janice we were in big trouble: Up to now, she and I had been able to avoid having to join the black socially elite clubs such as the Links, the Carousels, the Guardsmen and Jack and Jill. The wedding story in Ebony featuring me as Ron's best man would change all that.

Ron got back to the States the first week of March and moved into the Gatewood Apartments in the Old Town section of Petersville. The Gatewood, a turn-of-the-century structure, consisted of six, 3,000-square-foot apartment units. Lyzette spent a mint re-decorating their apartment. With the wedding and honeymoon out of the way, it was time to get back to the campaign.

Except for an occasional press conference called by the opposition to nitpick at Ron's performance in office, the campaign was quiet through June.

Then the attacks became more vicious.

Dwyer blamed Ron for every problem in Petersville. Ron's only response was to point to his record. The more negative Dwyer's attack, the more positive was Ron's response.

Dwyer's strategy was to demonize Ron to the white voters. Unfortunately for him, it was having the opposite effect on the black voters. The attacks galvanized the Southend Independent Democrats.

The SIA held its monthly meetings on the fourth Thursday at the Southend Waiters Club. There were more than 2,000 paid members of the SIA but before Dwyer's attacks on Ron, fewer than 200 people would attend. The SIA published a monthly newsletter that was mailed to each paid member. When Dwyer began his negative ad campaign, attendance at the June meeting increased to more than 500. SIA members were outraged at the nastiness of the attacks.

Since its inception, Ron had missed only one SIA meeting. That was the February meeting, when he was on his honeymoon.

The timing of the June meeting was perfect. It was the weekend before Ron's official campaign kickoff and the formal opening of his campaign headquarters. After completing all of the SIA's routine business, Ron was asked to report on the status of his campaign.

As he rose and walked to the podium, the crowd went wild, giving him a standing ovation that lasted almost five minutes. After everyone calmed down, Ron introduced Lyzette, who stood up and waved to more applause. Then she whispered something in his ear. Ron smiled and proceeded to talk.

He outlined why he should be re-elected. He cited the basics: Reduction in crime during his tenure, increased number of convictions and his basic anti-crime speech. Then he talked about why Dwyer and the other white Democrats wanted him out.

146

"When I came into office four years ago, the face of crime was black. My predecessor spent most of his time prosecuting drug-users and the victims of crime. The real perpetrators, the people who were bringing in the heroin, cocaine and marijuana on boats and planes from Mexico, South America and wherever else were not being aggressively prosecuted.

"My predecessor would hold press conferences highlighting drug-busts that were only scratching the surface of the drug business. The first thing I decided to do was to form an organized crime task force to root out the real drug-dealers."

"Not long after that, you all know what happened: The people who did not want any light shed on themselves attempted to quiet me with a bullet. But thanks to the good Lord and my friend Meat, (at that point, Ron grabbed Meat and pulled him to podium and embraced him), they missed."

The crowd erupted in another standing ovation, this one lasting two minutes. Ron had them right where he wanted them.

"The theme of my election is The Last Hurrah," Ron continued. *"The Last Hurrah"* was a novel that took its story from the life of the late President John F. Kennedy's grandfather, who was the first Irish Catholic Mayor of Boston. The central figure in the story is an elected official who stayed in office too long and lost touch with his changing constituency. Here in Petersville, the foes of inclusion have been there too long, and they have lost touch. This election is the last hurrah for cronyism. It is also the last hurrah for exclusion."

That speech set the tone for the rest of Ron's campaign. At the Campaign Kick-Off, an overflow crowd heard the same speech. The mainstream press could not ignore it. The size of the crowd had to be reported.

Yet even with all this momentum for Ron building, his opponents were not fazed. They continued a heavy barrage of

147

negative campaigning. The more they attacked, the more volunteers showed up at our headquarters.

Ron initially thought he would have to raise about $70,000 for his campaign; a lot of money for a citywide campaign in 1973. But the response from the SIA members and the entire black community was overwhelming, so he did have not worry too much about money.

Ron's campaign headquarters was on the eastern edge of downtown Petersville. The building was a large vacant furniture store with huge plate glass windows out front. Ron had covered most of the plate-glass front of the building with his large pictures of himself and campaign signs.

I tried to come by the office and work whenever I could. Ron did not allow anyone to be excused from working, including and *especially* his friends and family. I remember the first time I saw Lyzette there. One day I was driving by the headquarters and saw Ron's car parked out front and decided to stop and visit with him. Ron was on the phone, trying to raise money. Lyzette was at a receptionist desk.

"Hello sir," she chirped, in her accent, a cross between New York and Jamaica. "May I help you?"

"Isn't anything sacred to this man?" I laughed. "He even talked you into working for him."

"He didn't talk me into doing anything; this is my idea," she stated proudly with her head. I wanted to know exactly what it is my man does and the best way is to work here and see for myself. Ron actually tried to talk me out of it."

"It is called the power of suggestion. I'll bet he didn't try very hard."

"Leave my wife alone," Ron bellowed from the other side of the room. "She is the best volunteer I have."

"Thank you, Ronnie," Lyzette said as they embraced and kissed.

"The honeymoon is still in effect," I said. "That's good. Try and make it last for as long as you can."

"Come on, Billy," Ron said, putting his arm around my shoulder and guiding me back behind two swinging doors. "Let me show you why I'm going to win. This is the war room."

Behind the doors was a beehive of at least 50 people sitting in chairs and making phone calls at tables lined up against the walls. Each wall was papered with maps of all the wards and precincts in the city.

"I have 30 telephones, and we are calling *every* registered voter in the eight wards favorable to me. Each household is going to be called at least three times before the election, and every one of them will be called at least twice on Election Day. At first, I was only going to install 20 telephones, but the response from the call for volunteers has been so overwhelming, I decided to install 10 more."

"How did you get the phone numbers?" I asked.

"I got a copy of a cross-reference book published by the phone company and matched it up with the registered voter lists supplied by the election board. It took 50 college students working eight hours a day in May to get it done. We have another crew that prepares the literature for mailing. I'll mail every registered voter in the predominately-black wards at least three times."

"What about the white wards and the integrated wards?"

"I think Dwyer's negative campaigning will polarize most of the white voters against me. My strategy is to let sleeping dogs lie. I believe that by not mailing to the white voters, I can create the false impression that I don't have a lot of money. I'm hoping this will make some of the voters think that Dwyer is a shoo-in and get lazy and decide not to vote."

"The voter registration rolls indicate the city is split right down the middle: 50 percent white and 50 percent black. Unfortunately, the white voter turnout is 20-30 percent higher than the black voter turnout. If I can generate a 70 percent black turnout, I can match Dwyer vote-for-vote. Add in the 3-5 percent white vote I'll get and I win 52 to 48 percent!"

"This is an expensive operation. Where will the money come from?"

"That's something you don't' want to know," Ron said, quickly dismissing further questions on the subject of money. It's legal, though."

There were no laws then requiring reports on who-gave-what and how the campaign funds were spent, so I let it go.

"It is an impressive operation," I said as I scanned the room full of people working.

"If this works out," Ron cautiously offered, "I'm going to keep it in place, so I won't have to spend so much time gearing-up again."

"You won't have to gear up for another four years," I said. "How do you figure you can keep this group motivated for that long?"

"Who says it will be that long?" Ron beamed and walked back to the reception area. "I've got a half-hour before my next meeting, and I'm going to spend it with my bride." Ron left me almost choking to death from curiosity.

I left Ron's headquarters confident he was on top of things. My feeling was justified in August when he defeated Dwyer by the exact percentage-point difference he had predicted.

Ron had created a grassroots organization that put 200 paid workers on the street to canvass door-to-door in targeted, low-turnout precincts. There were 150 more workers at polling sites on Election Day. The result was a 78 percent turnout of the black vote.

Dwyer was so upset that he charged vote fraud. On the night of the election, Dwyer was quoted as saying the turnout was unprecedented and "had a pungent aroma of impropriety."

Ron fired off a press release condemning Dwyer's comments as racist: "When blacks vote for white Democrats, you don't hear the cry of fraud from white elected officials. It is only when blacks vote and elect black candidates that fraud is cited as the reason for the victory."

Several white Democratic officials, unwilling to accept the defeat of their Great White Hope, filed a formal complaint with the election board that alleged numerous instances of voter fraud. They also asked the board to delay certifying the election results.

Since it was the governor who appointed the Board of Election Commissioners, Ron asked him to convince the commissioners to kill the investigation request. Ron suggested that any fraud investigation by a Democratic-controlled board could upset black voters and that could have a negative effect on the November general elections.

The governor agreed. He was protecting his pork chops because he was on the ballot in a tough race in November and did not want to upset the black voter base. There was no investigation. Since no Republican had filed for the DA job, Ron would run unopposed in November.

CHAPTER 16

I thought Ron would take some time off after the grueling re-election fight, but he was up early the next morning. I was used to him calling me early but since we were both up late the night before celebrating his primary victory, I was looking forward to sleeping late. Ron called me at 6am. I let the phone ring at least ten times hoping whoever was calling would get the hint that it was too early.

On the eleventh ring I answered. "Good morning Ron. You are the only person I know who would let a phone ring ten times and not take the hint that the person on the other end is either not available and doesn't want to talk. What in the world can't wait until later this morning? I am dog-tired, and you should be tired too."

"It is time to start planning to consummate the deal," Ron said chuckling.

"What deal? You just made history for the second time in four years being the first black District Attorney in the United States to get elected not once, but twice."

"I know you don't really believe that is what this is all about... being the DA? This is just step one in our quest to get the power to change the quality of life for black people in Petersville. The Mayoral election is next spring. We don't have a lot of time to organize; less than six months."

Unbothered by my talking on the phone this early, Janice was used to Ron calling me at *all* times of day and night. "You won't be sworn in as DA until January and will be running for Mayor at the same time?"

"Before you get bent out of shape over something that ultimately you are going to understand and support, brush your teeth, get dressed and meet me at the diner on 9th Street for breakfast. I don't want you to wake Jan up and I start losing votes before the campaign starts."

Reluctantly I crawled out and bed and got dressed and did what he suggested.

The diner on 9th Street, which was also its name, was a favorite of so-called white progressives in the democratic party in Petersville. They gave a lot of lip service and support to black people who could talk proper and "modulate their tone," but always found a reason to not support sharing real power with black democrats. Except for a few of them and I mean a *very few*, they all supported Dwyer against Ron. When confronted on the reason they did not support Ron, the answer would be his tone and he was impatient. What that meant to me is they did not want to support someone who would make them unwelcome and uncomfortable at the Thanksgiving dinner table with their parents and other white relatives. As I have grown older I have become more tolerant and respectful of their white relatives who were honest about their racism as opposed to the so-called white liberals.

Ron was already eating breakfast when I arrived. He poured me a cup of coffee, with this big grin on his face said softly and slyly, "What's up my brother?" This should have been my signal to run because Ron had already written the play and was meeting with me to tell me what my role was going to be.

The waitress came over and I ordered the American breakfast. For some reason I had developed an appetite. When she left the table, Ron wasted no time.

"I am going to announce at the September meeting of the SIA for Mayor. Before you start telling me why it is *not* a good idea, let me tell you my reasoning."

Leaning forward in my chair I wanted to make sure I heard every word as to how he was going to spin this yarn to the voters. With a presidential and gubernatorial election in November, and Ron just getting re-elected DA, what would be the justification for running for Mayor before being sworn in as District Attorney and explain away the obvious charge that all of this wasn't some Machiavellian power-grabbing scheme.

With a big smile of his face, Ron pushed several typed pages across the table, "This is a draft of the announcement speech I am going to give to SIA. Read it and let me know what you think."

"The re-election campaign for DA was just a trial run," Ron said nonchalantly as he resumed eating his breakfast.

While he ate. I read the two-page speech and one page of bullet points. His rationale for running was a declaration of war on the City democratic party. Ron cited a list of grievances most of them centered on a longstanding complaint among black elected officials and community leaders about the unwillingness of the white democratic establishment to share power. He cited employment, allocation of city services and police brutality as the primary issues he would address if he were elected.

"It is a good speech, but we are going to need more than a good speech to handle the pushback from the democratic establishment. They are already pissed at how you hijacked the DA job. Now you are going to run for Mayor?"

"We are not going to win playing by their rules and trying to effect change through incrementalism," Ron shot back. "What do we have to lose? Black people on the Southend have be voting lock step with the Democrats since 1932, and what have we got? The current party leaders are against everything we propose. They boldly attend white citizens council meetings. They are opposed to affirmative action programs. The city council did not pass a public accommodations bill until last year and that was because the only two Republicans on the 21-member city council voted for it. We have population for at least 8 wards that could elect a black to the City Council, but only have five due to gerrymandering by the "white" Democrats. So, my redundant question is: What do we have to lose?"

"I don't disagree with any of the issues you cite; I am just concerned that you could lose and if by chance you win, we will be trading one office for another. Wasn't it you who said the DA is the elected office that impacts black and poor people the most?"

"I still believe that *and* I have a plan to make sure the DA's office stays in the hands of a black lawyer."

"How? Last time I checked the power to appoint your successor resides in the state capitol with the Governor. That sounds like a problem. The Governor is sure to appoint a white boy as your replacement."

"Under normal situations I would agree with," Ron said with a boyish smirk that he always had on his face when he had outwitted someone.

"I helped the Governor out with a problem his son had. His son had a car accident that almost killed someone. He was tested and was charged with driving under the influence. I had the charges suppressed and his record expunged in a sealed court proceeding."

"What makes you feel you can trust the Governor to not fuck you?"

"Trust me on this, he won't."

"Let's get past the 20 questions. I know you have already made up your mind about whom you want. So just tell me who it is."

"You."

I started laughing, first thinking that Ron was joking. I quickly realized that he was serious. One of Ron's problems was his lack of a sense of humor.

"I'm serious," Ron said as he leaned over to fill my coffee cup. "I cannot think of anyone that I trust more and respect more than you. And you meet the qualifications."

"I haven't been in a courtroom in almost four years. The press and your enemies will kill me on the experience issue and my closeness to you."

"They will initially, but you will have almost three and a half years to get over that. Plus, you have been my chief assistant for four years. You know better than most that the DA's job is mostly ministerial. Your friendship with me will be a plus in a large segment of the Petersville community."

"I'm not sure I am the right person, Ron. You have the disposition that a politician needs. While the intrigue and treachery of politics excites you, it is a turn off to me. Plus, I don't know what Jan will say. I appreciate your thinking of me, but I don't that I would be a good choice."

"You don't have to decide today. I won't be sworn in as Mayor until next April," Ron said.

"It will not take me that long to decide. I will talk it over with Jan today."

As I drove home from our meeting, what seemed at first to be something that I thought I would never want to do, was becoming more intriguing. Ron had stimulated my ego and ambition just enough for me to give serious consideration to his proposal. Pulling up to my apartment, the initial feeling of euphoria faded when I thought about Janice. I did not have a clue what her response would be. The baby had brought additional expenses that did not help our finances, but we were making ends meet. Janice was giving the baby a bath when I walked in.

"How was the meeting with Machiavelli?" she asked bent over the tub wiping the baby off. Notwithstanding the few pounds she had put on since the baby, my woman was still a looker. Bent over the tub, the sight of her perfectly shaped ass still got me excited. I began thinking about the times before the baby came that I would come home and we would engage in spontaneous and robust sex.

"Billy did you hear me?

"I'm sorry baby. Seeing you bent over the tub like that gave me a flashback. The meeting was well attended."

"You need to do something about that flashback. I don't want people to think you are senile," she said wiggling her butt to tease me.

"No problemo mamasita. As fast as you can put that curtain puller and crumb snatcher to bed, I will accommodate you request."

"Stop that. I got six miles to walk in the house before I can get to sleep. What did Ron want to talk about?"

"The Mayor's race, or as he puts it, his moment with destiny."

"What was so urgent about that, that he had to meet with you so early?

"He told me he is going to announce for Mayor next month and he wants me to succeed him as DA." Janice was holding the baby in her hands when I said that and I had to grab her arms to keep her from dropping him. She sat down on the commode and just stared at me. After about ten seconds she composed herself and responded in a most unpredictable way.

"You told him yes didn't you?

"No, I told him that I would have to talk to you first."

"That's real sweet honey, but you did give him a qualified yes predicated upon my response right?"

"No. I told him that I needed to talk it over with you first."

"OK. I agree. Call him right now and tell him yes before he offers to someone else."

"Just like that? Don't you think we need to talk about it first?"

"What is there to talk about? You know as much about politics as Ron does. You have been with him since the beginning and the people know and respect you. That is why you have a wife and partner."

"I am really surprised that you are so supportive of the idea of me being an elected official."

"The one thing I agree with Ron about is this destiny thing. We are at the right place and the right time. If Ron leaves the DA's office without finding a replacement to continue his reform efforts, things will revert back before the next election. And why shouldn't you be a beneficiary of the spoils you and Ron helped create? Go for it baby, I got your back."

"Finish putting the baby to bed so I can get some of your back."

Obeying my wife, I called Ron and told him I was in.

***

The September meeting of SIA was the first meeting after his primary election victory and the SIA members were there in full force to celebrate. The crowd was probably the largest to ever attend a meeting at the Waiters Club. Ron got Rita to introduce him.

Rita gave a rousing intro, citing Ron's record and commitment. Rita became emotional when she started to talk about the attempt on Ron's life.

"The same evil forces that killed my son, tried to kill Ron. But without hesitation Ron stepped up and said not today Satan. This is the kind of leader we need. Someone fearless and not afraid to fight for us. For too many years the people who controlled the Democratic party took our vote for granted. Ron was born and raised right here in the South End. He is for us and we need to show him he is for us. So, I present to some and present to others Ron Jackson, the next Mayor of the city of Petersville." You could hear a pin drop. The silence was broken when a loud thundering voice started chanting "Run, Ron, Run!" over and over again.

As Ron stepped up to podium, the number of people chanting had become a crescendo of the crowd standing and clapping. Ron approached the podium, in what was a perfectly rehearsed, look of humility in (what was obvious to me) a staged event. But it was working as Ron was getting what he wanted. About thirty seconds into the chanting, Ron was waving his hands motioning the crowd.

He tried to get them to stop, but the crowd just kept on going. Ron stepped down from the podium and came back to his chair. As he was passing me, I whispered in his ear, "Nice going; it even looked spontaneous. What better way to decide to run for Mayor than to have your constituents draft you."

Word about Ron's plans to run for Mayor was being widely criticized by the press and other politicians. They said he should not have run for DA if he knew he was going to run for Mayor. Most of the criticism was coming from Dwyer and political associates of the Mayor. Ron let the criticism run like water off a duck's back. Ron had decided to wait until February to formally announce his intentions. He decided to wait until then for two reasons. One was the fact that his swearing in ceremony was the first week of January. The other reason was a story that Look Magazine was doing on the influence of organized crime within big city government. The story was scheduled to hit the newsstand in February. Ron had been interviewed about the Syrians influence in Petersville and the writer had brought up the Mayor's name in connection with his relationship with the Syrians. The Mayor, Roberto Salazar, was married to Bobby Saleem's sister. Saleem was the late Ansur Thomas's nephew. Saleem was a real estate developer and childhood friend of Salazar's who had received millions of dollars in subsidy from the city for his development projects. Additionally, a company co-owned by him had just recently been awarded an exclusive franchise to provide cable TV to the city of Petersville. The other co-owners were Thomas Conroy, a powerful labor leader who had ties to organized crime, and, the late Ansur Thomas. Ron was going to use the timing of the article as justification for his decision to challenge Salazar. It was a stretch, but it would provide some cover from the criticism that he was an opportunist.

Ron decided to have his swearing in ceremony on New Year's Day. For effect, he had the ceremony performed in the Petersville City Hall rotunda. He was getting less and less subtle about his intentions. Since Wiley had decided to fly in from New York, we decided to hold a reunion of our gang on New Year's Eve. Ron offered to host the party at his apartment. Lyzette had prepared an African American traditional New Year's meal of black-eyed peas, chitterlings and hog head sausage served

160

with Moet Chandon champagne and Remy Martin Napoleon cognac. She added a roasted chicken entrée that she made for those of us who were beginning to spread a little at the waist. She then left to go and visit Ron's parents. Ron had invited T.C. this time so the old gang was back together again. Ron got up and made the first toast.

"To our man Snake. There is not a day that goes by that I don't think about you brother," Ron said as he hoisted his glass to the sky. Wiley followed with a toast to Ron's successful re-election efforts.

"To the baddest nigger politician I know," Wiley said raising his champagne flute in Ron's direction. The rest of us responded in like form.

"I would like to make another toast," T.C. said getting up and walking over to Wiley. "This is probably more of an announcement than a toast. To C and F Vending, on our way to making a boat load of cash."

"Wiley pulled it off. He arranged the financing for us. We owe everything to him."

"What is C and F Vending?" Leonard responded.

"It is a joint venture between T.C. and I," Wiley shot back. "Last year when the Syrians were killing each other off, Ron called and told me about a business opportunity that had developed. The Syrians had controlled the vending business on the Southend for years through intimidation and fear. He thought this would be an excellent time for a well-funded black vending company to emerge."

"And the fact that the DA's office was indicting seven members of the family that controlled the vending business did not play a part in your decision?" I interjected with a smirk on my face.

"Damn Betsy; it did," T.C. answered giving me a hand slap. "Some niggers tried to do the same thing in 1964. You do remember the Crandall brothers, Ronnell and Noble? They were both shot down with a hail of bullets coming out of the Living Room."

"I called Wiley for two reasons," Ron interjected. "One was I wanted to try and convince him to come back to Petersville and the other was to bring our friend T.C. out of the cold."

"What do the initials stand for?" I asked.

"Chambers and Fentress. Although it should be Fentress and Chambers given the value of what I do compared to Wiley."

"Don't let T.C. tell y'all that shit. He had a good business plan that I was able to sell."

"And put your money into."

"Money I intend to get a return on. Friendship got us to talking, money is what got the deal done."

"Just what do you do now Wiley? Billy was telling me that you have changed jobs," Ron interrupted.

"I am still an investment banker. I start to work for Brooks and Company on January 15th. They hired me to head up their municipal finance department. Brooks is an old brokerage and securities firm that was bought out by some of its former employees. They see a trend developing where blacks are becoming the voting authority in a large number of urban cities. As a consequence, a number of these cities, like Atlanta, Detroit, Newark and Cleveland are electing black mayors and blacks to the city councils. Most of the municipal finance that is done in this country is done in the cities."

"What in the hell is municipal finance?" Leonard interrupted to ask.

162

"It is the way state and local governments borrow money. A state or city government or local governmental agency issue and sell tax-exempt bonds to raise the money it needs for capital improvements and cash to pay for municipal services. Companies like Brooks provide consultant and underwriting services to these local and state governments a fee. A very generous fee I might add. I did a 100-million-dollar bond deal for the city of Newark last week and charged them 4 million dollars," Wiley responded.

"How much do you make off a deal like that?"

"I get a salary plus a year-end bonus based on the revenue I generate in a given year."

"So you are going to be the stalking horse they use to get these cities now controlled by blacks to hire them to issue their debt," Ron added with a smirk.

"That's it in a nutshell."

"The first initial act I will make as Mayor is to hire your company to serve as the city's financial consultant."

"Mayor? You are running for Mayor?" Leonard yelled, almost falling out his chair.

"That's correct. I will be announcing it formally around the first of February."

Everyone got up and walked over to shake Ron's hand except T.C. He conspicuously stayed seated as Ron accepted the backslapping and handshaking approvals from the rest of us. T.C. remained seated there motionless with his face frowning, not hiding his displeasure.

Neither Ron nor T.C. said anything and no one else had noticed him until I looked and saw that he had not got up. I walked over to him and gave him a glass of champagne.

"He thinks they gave him a hard time as DA, he ain't nothing like the pressure he will get as Mayor," T.C. mumbled as he gulped down the flute of champagne.

The Mayor of Petersville controlled all of the real significant patronage. The city council was a check, but it was only one vote shy of a black majority and most of the blacks belonged to the SIA and were candidates groomed by Ron. Salazar was in his third term as Mayor and had been a model for how a Mayor can use the power of his office to control everything. Other than T.C.'s comments, the rest of us were ready to assume our place in history.

CHAPTER 17

The *Look Magazine* articles on Salazar hit the newsstand the first week of February. The reporter who wrote the story sent Ron an advanced copy of the unedited story that had items that had to be left out because of libel implications. The article alleged that Salazar had been recruited and groomed by the Syrians from the time he was in high school. His father had emigrated to the U.S. from Spain in the 1930's, fleeing the Spanish Civil war. He had been an attorney in Spain and was lured to Petersville by a distant cousin who was an associate of Ansur Thomas. His father got a job working on the riverfront for a trucking firm owned by Ansur Thomas. The elder Salazar went to night law school while studying to become an American citizen. It took him ten years to do both. By then he had become a vice president of the trucking firm and a close associate and friend of Saleem. This association with the Syrians flowed down to his son who was born in the U.S. He followed his father and also became a lawyer. He became a close friend of Saleem's son and married one of Saleem's daughters.

Mayor Salazar's first entry into politics began right after he graduated from law school. He was appointed to the city council to replace a Syrian City councilman that had died. The article did not cite any specific instances of wrong doing by Salazar, but the inferences drawn through examples of how patronage was dispersed to the Syrians were strong and damaging. It also showed pictures of Salazar on vacation at Las Vegas hotels owned by Ansur Thomas's brother. Ansur's brother bought the hotel using a loan from the Teamsters Union. This was also in the *Look Magazine* article. The article questioned how Ansur's brother was able to borrow 10 million to buy a casino on the salary of a court clerk.

The expose gave Ron the public story he needed to tell to justify his decision to run. He had a reputation of being a fair-minded and honest prosecutor, untouched by scandal. His strategy was to use this to pull progressive liberal votes away from Salazar. This had been a strong base for Salazar in the past. Shortly after the *Look Magazine* articles surfaced, a group calling themselves the Petersville Citizens for Honest Government, held a press conference calling for Salazar's resignation. *The Gazette* printed an editorial that blasted Mayor Salazar for his associations, but stopped short of asking him to resign. Ron was able to get some of the members of the Honest Government Group, as well as the SIA to attend his announcement press conference.

The timing and depth of the *Look Magazine* articles could not be dismissed as mere aggressive journalism. It was clear that someone had given the writers a road map showing them where to look. When the announcement press conference was winding down, I walked over to Ron and whispered, "This shit was brilliant."

He turned quickly and looked at me, initially with a frown of his face; when his eyes met mine, he lowered his head momentarily and smiled to acknowledge that I had peeped him.

The campaign was almost like sleepwalking. Salazar was mortally wounded; he could do nothing to counter the feeling among a large percentage of voters that he was controlled by organized crime. *The Gazette* did a seven-day follow-up expose detailing additional contractual and business relationship between Salazar, Saleem and people identified by the paper as associates of organized crime. The incumbent Mayor spent most of his time on the defensive.

The bad publicity notwithstanding, Ron won by a narrow margin of less than 1 percent. The white voters on the Northside were still not going to vote for a nigger under any circumstances. Ron performed extremely well among the progressive whites and there was another record turnout of black voters spurred on by the prospect of electing Petersville's first black Mayor. In just seven years, Ron had gone from a ward committeeman to Mayor.

The black community treated his victory like a coronation. Pride swelled in the hearts of the average black person who saw Ron's victory as a testament to the years of struggle for civil rights. While I was happy that Ron won, his winning also had meaning for me. I was still dubious of his ability to get the Governor to appoint me as his successor in the DA's office. However, what I failed to realize at the time was another consequence of Ron's victory. He had suddenly become the number one black Democrat in the state, which in turn, made him the titular head of the most loyal Democrats in the Democratic Party. All roads to success for a Democratic candidate in the state ran through Ron.

The Governor had called Ron at the campaign headquarters the night of the election. He congratulated him and scheduled a meeting for the following week. The meeting was in Ron's office in the Circuit Court Building. The Governor was playing it as courtesy call, but it was really a face-to-face between the two most powerful democrats in the state. Ron asked me to attend the meeting to meet the Governor so we could cut the deal to have my appointment as his successor that day. The mayoral general election was three weeks away and no Republican candidate had filed. Ron wanted to get the Governor's support for my appointment as his successor before the election.

The press had been camped outside the courthouse all morning waiting on the Governor. The Governor's press people wanted to make sure that the meeting got wide coverage on the local news. Petersville was the largest TV market in the state and this was an excellent opportunity for the Governor to get some free airtime. Accompanying him was his chief of staff, campaign consultant, and legal counsel. After congratulating Ron and sharing with us a good old boy joke, he and Ron got right down to business.

"First I want to thank you for the consideration you gave my son. His mother told me to thank you also," the governor stated as his beginning remarks.

"I hope he is doing okay now," Ron replied.

"He understands that he dodged a bullet and I think I made him appreciate the value of the consideration you extended him. Now, to the first matter of interest. My staff and I have reviewed the credentials of Mr. Strayhorn and they find him to be a little wet behind the ears. Are you sure this is the person you want appointed to succeed you?"

"Yes, wet ears and all. He is the person I believe will best serve the interests of the entire Petersville community."

"You know I have received a lot of resumes from a number of my friends. There will be uproar if I appoint Strayhorn. I am getting a lot of pressure from northside politicians who think I should appoint Ed Dwyer, Jr. as your successor."

"We both know that is not an acceptable choice. You appoint Billy and you can automatically bank 40,000 votes in this city for a city or state- wide Democratic candidate. That is how you can justify the appointment to yourself. You can call it enlightened self-interest."

"The Governor will not be able to win with just the black votes," a skinny Robert Hall suit-wearing white boy, a campaign aid for the Governor, chimed in.

"And he cannot win without them," I offered as I reached out to shake the Governor's hand. "My name is Billy Strayhorn," I said.

"The man of the hour" the Governor responded.

"Thank you, sir."

"Listen Ron," the Governor said getting up and walking towards the window. "You got a room someplace close by where we can talk alone?"

Ron picked up his telephone and dialed the intercom. "Margaret, would you check and see if my conference room is available?"

"I had it cleared already just in case you needed it," Margaret responded.

"Let's go next door Governor; we can have some privacy in my conference room."

Ron and the governor went through a door that led to his conference room.

"Damn son, your office is almost as large as mine. I may have run for the wrong office."

"Tell that to the wall Governor," Ron shot back as he closed the door. They were in there together for about 15 minutes, although it seemed like two hours. When they emerged both men were smiling.

"I will tell the press that we had a productive meeting and that we talked about how we could both work together as public officials and democrats to improve the quality of life of the residents of Petersville. Does that sound ok?"

"Perfect," Ron said. "I will mimic your statement and no more when I talk to them this afternoon."

"I think I am going to like doing business with you, Mr. Jackson."

"Call me Ron, Governor."

"Only if you stop saying Governor."

The two men shook hands and Ron escorted the Governor to the hallway door. I stayed in Ron's office pacing like an expectant father until he came back.

"Well what's up?

"Congratulations Mr. DA. It's a done deal. He will appoint you the day after I am sworn in. It seems that he wants to run for the U.S. Senate so we did some horse-trading. There is also a history of bad blood between him and Dwyer and he thinks that Dwyer wants to run for Governor. The good old boys don't want to help him build a base. Ambition is a powerful force. It made allies out of me and a redneck from Richardson County."

"I've got to call Janice. I told her that I would call her as soon as I knew something. Thanks bro."

"Shit, thank *you*. We did it Billy. You were the person who believed in me from day one. And it is not over yet. Now we have to deliver. Petersville is getting ready to get the best government it has ever had."

***

The general election was held almost a month to the day later. The white Democrats put up a write-in candidate that made Ron have to campaign a little. The vote was 75 percent to 25 percent. The State and National Democratic Party pumped in money and organizational support that made it impossible for Ron to lose. The swearing in ceremony was scheduled exactly three weeks later. Because of the historic nature of electing the first black mayor, more than five thousand people attended the ball that was held at the Petersville convention center. The SIA held another private "Invitation Only" celebration at the Waiters Club. We had two things to celebrate that night. Ron's victory and the Governor keeping his word and announcing my appointment as DA. I had three years left to try and get myself re-elected. As was expected the press fed by the white Democrats denounced the appointment and called it a political deal. The Governor, to his credit, was steadfast and responded that yes it was a political deal. That's what most politicians are elected to do.

True to his promise to give Petersville the best government it had ever had, Ron announced during his inauguration speech some sweeping changes he was going to propose. The one that was the most controversial was his proposal to get rid of the patronage system. "No more political jobs" was his mantra. He rattled off a list of reforms he was going to institute to "bring Petersville into the 20th century." The press and the public loved it. The elected officials went bonkers. Ron was going to use reform to make the Mayor's office stronger and more powerful at the expense of the ward politicians. It was ironic that he wanted to reform the same system he exploited with skill and deftness to get to the Mayor office. He told me that he wanted to make it harder for anyone to use the same roadmap to take him out.

CHAPTER 18

I was sworn in as the District Attorney the next day. I immediately scheduled a meeting with the attorneys and support staff of the office. Anticipating that some of the staff might be upset about my appointment, I confronted the issue head on. I sent out a memo that allowed anyone who had anything to say to speak or forever hold his or her peace. I also told the staff that I was only going to entertain comments this one time and that if any of them did not feel comfortable working for me, they could leave now with no hard feelings. A few of the lawyers expressed concern about the transition. I told them that should not be a problem because for the immediate future there would be no changes in personnel. This seemed to satisfy most of them.

While I was fumbling around trying to get comfortable as the new DA, Ron hit the ground running. He sent out letters asking for the resignations of all the appointed members of the different Petersville city governing boards of which he was the appointing authority. He was going to put his stamp on the operations that the Mayor controlled as fast as he could. He got Wiley's firm to provide an analysis of Petersville's financial health. They were more than willing to do it because it could mean business for them. Ron took office April 20th and the city charter required that the city's budget had to be presented to the city council by May 1st. This put Ron at an extremely precarious position. His transition team had received very little help from Salazar's staff.

Most of them had resigned before the 20th. Wiley came in and assembled a staff to prepare the budget. He had a budget prepared and submitted to the city council in ten days. Ron and I took Wiley to dinner to celebrate. I was curious as to how he was able to prepare a budget for the city that quick. Wiley just laughed as he ordered a beer from our waiter.

"I looked at the last three years of city budgets and determined what the average rate of revenue growth was and increased each line item in this fiscal year's budget by one half of whatever the average percentage growth was. The average had been four percent, so I increased the budget by two percent."

"That is some simple but brilliant shit," I said as I reached out my hand to give him a congratulatory hand slap.

"The beauty of the theory, if it plays out the way I planned it, is that the conservative under-estimation of revenue will give the city a budget surplus next year," Wiley continued.

"That is the kind of shit that will get me re-elected," Ron interjected. "I really do appreciate what you did. I wish there was a way for you to stay on, but the city cannot afford you."

"Ever since you told me you were running for Mayor, I have been trying to find a way to come home and I believe I have found it. My father has developed something the doctors are calling premature senility and my mother cannot take care of him. I will either have to put him in a home or hire someone to take care of him. Either of those scenarios will require me to spend more time here. Plus, I am tired of the traveling and I do not think the other partners at Brooks are ever going to make me a partner. They look at public finance as being all-political and requiring no skills. This brings me to the deal I am trying to put together to buy the South End National Bank."

"You are trying to buy a bank?" I felt almost embarrassed asking the question. I had never thought about how much money

Wiley made. "I know the question sounds patronizing but I don't know any black people who can buy a bank."

"Don't feel pregnant. Everybody responds the same way."

"I think it a great idea. What can I do to help?" Ron asked with a smile on his face that clearly expressed his enthusiasm.

"Hold that thought. It is going to take me about a year to finalize, if it can be done. The bank is for sale and I am preparing an offer sheet. The white boys who own it want to move to the county to follow their customers. They are having a problem getting a charter. This is where you can help me Ron. If I can get them a charter for a new bank they will sell me South End National at a discount."

"Fuck that, why not get your own charter. That way you don't have to buy any of their baggage. South End was the bank that the NAACP picketed last year because of their discriminatory hiring practices."

"That is the best deal. I just did not know if I could get a charter."

"If I can get them a charter, I can get you one."

"There is no way a black bank would not do well," I interrupted. "You would get all the black banking business in town."

"Don't take this the wrong way Billy, but no bank can survive on just being a black bank. It would end up being nothing more than a currency exchange. Black businesses fail every day because instead of having a business plan as the basis for survival, they had a civil rights plan. I will go after all the consumer business I can handle. I will also be talking to my friend, the "Mayor" about some institutional accounts. The city currently does all of its banking at Petersville 1st National. As the custodian of the city's pension funds, they receive .05 percent of the total amount of the fund annually. The three city pension

174

funds are valued at 1 billion dollars. They also manage the investments of the pension for an annual fee of .05 percent. That is an annual combined total of ten million dollars for last year alone. I just want ten percent of what they do."

"First things first. It will take me at least a year to get a charter."

"How much money do you need for initial capitalization?" Ron interjected.

"That is the right question. Each state's requirements are different. Then there are the federal requirements. I have about a million dollars of my own money that I plan to use to capitalize it with. I will sell stock eventually, but I intend to keep a controlling interest."

"One million dollars? Goddamn that is a lot of money. You made that as an investment banker?" I asked.

"I have been bringing in close to a million dollars in revenue to the firm for the past three years. Last year I brought in five million dollars. I receive a salary plus a bonus that is supposed to be at least ten percent of the revenue I generate. I have been living off my salary and my expense account and banking my bonus. It is actually more like 1.2 million. So I can afford to start a bank."

"Now I see why you were so anxious to work on the city budget. You have become extremely familiar with all of the city's banking needs," Ron said smiling and shaking his head.

"Yes sir. I can save the city a lot of money and I can make a lot of money legitimately. It will also help our politics to have a friendly banker."

"Just let me know what I need to do," Ron said. "I would like to continue this conversation, but I have got to go. I need to go home and see my wife."

***

I spent the first weeks in the DA office honing up on the legal and constitutional responsibilities of the DA. I also enrolled in a seminar at Harvard for new prosecutors. In addition, I decided to personally select a few cases to prosecute. Nothing could substitute for firsthand knowledge of what prosecuting a case would be like. One day while rummaging through one of Ron's old file cabinets, I ran across a file in a blank folder. When I opened it, I recognized the name in the file immediately. It was George Martin's file. George had been dead for almost seven years and all anyone could say about who killed him was speculative. It was always assumed that the Syrians killed him, but with most of their organization's major players either dead or in jail, because of their 1970 gang war, it was difficult to verify that speculation. When Ron first got elected I had asked him to let me do a review of the case. He told me that he would do a review but that he did not think I should be the one to do it. He stated that he thought both he and I were too close to the case and thus could not maintain the level of objectivity needed to do a fair job. I remember telling him "Fuck fairness. Let's just do to them what they would do to us." I lost the argument. I started reading the file and the more I read, the more intrigued I became with what was not in the file. There was no ballistic report in the file. The report said that George was shot with a high-powered large caliber rifle. It went on to say that the shooter was probably on a roof or in a window, several hundred feet away. The only bullets or casings found were the ones taken from George's body. The way George was shot brought to mind the assassination attempt on Ron. I asked my secretary to retrieve George's file for me. As I read his file, I found the investigation of the possible suspects quite interesting.

The report made reference to a tape that the FBI had as a result of a wiretap and or bugging of the Syrians' phone calls and conversations. The transcript of the tape was not in the file. I made note that numerous key items were interestingly absent from the file. I gave it to my secretary and told her to try and locate them for me.

A couple of weeks had passed when I remembered the request I had made of my secretary to locate some files that pertained to the George Martin case. It was a Monday morning when I asked Mrs. Metcalf what had happened to my request. She started looking and fumbling through some papers on her desk and without making eye contact with me mumbled some incoherent comment. Putting my hands on her desk, I leaned over to make sure she heard me and I could hear her response.

"I did not understand what you said. Would you mind repeating it?"

"I forgot sir. I have been so busy I did not get around to it."

"See if you can put it in your schedule to get them today. I want the files or a satisfactory reason why I don't have them before 5pm today."

"Yes Sir."

This was the first time I had been that stern with her. Primarily because I had been more than happy with her up until now. I did not think she was being honest with me. And if there is one thing I cannot tolerate, it is dishonesty or disloyalty.

I spent the rest of that Monday morning in meetings with my staff reviewing cases. Around 11:30am. I got a call from Ron asking me to have lunch with him. I did not have lunch plans and even if I did I would have changed them to accommodate the Mayor. He told me he was going to have lunch brought in because he was on a pretty tight schedule. The courts were directly across the street from City Hall making my trip to his office a five-minute walk.

I arrived at exactly noon and Meat immediately ushered me into his office. Meat, now the Mayor's scheduler, greeted me at the office door. He had retired from the police department and was receiving a disability pension as a result of the wounds he received protecting Ron from the assassination attempt. His official title was Administrative Assistant to the Mayor.

"Turkey or Ham and Swiss?

"Huh," I hesitated until I realized he was asking which type of sandwich I wanted for lunch.

"Turkey, turkey," I said punching Meat on his shoulder.

"Billy what's up? I will be with you in a minute," Ron yelled from the other side of the room. The Mayor's office always reminded me more of an art gallery or museum than an office. It had paintings that traced the history of the founding of Petersville everywhere. Written on the bottom of the frames were inscriptions that gave a historical antidote for each painting.

"I am going to take that one down and put up a picture of some of Petersville's African American historical figures," Ron whispered in my ear as he was escorting his guests out of his office.

The office could use some color, I thought to myself as I continued to browse. I did not have to wait long. Ron came in with Meat following him with two white boxes on a tray and two bottles of root beer.

"I know this is not the quality of lunch that you are accustomed to, but I thought you might want to try eating the way working people do," Ron laughed as he sat down at a table in the corner of his office.

"That's one thing I have learned since I took this job. Elected officials really don't have jobs. The founders of this country created politics to give the ruling class titles. Although they

178

rebelled against divine rule, they still wanted some type of caste system available to satisfy their egos."

"Now that is some deep shit. How did you get there from what I said?" Ron responded with an incredulous look on his face.

"Easy. I listen to all of these white conservative politicians talk about ending everybody's welfare but theirs. For some of these elected officials, the job they have now is the only job they have ever had. Yet, they have the audacity to complain about people who receive welfare or food stamps. I'll get off my soap box, what's up?"

"I got a call from a friend in the FBI telling me that you requested some wiretap and bugging transcripts from them concerning the George Martin case."

"And?"

"I was just curious as to why you are looking at that case," Ron said opening his box lunch and unwrapping his sandwich. I followed his lead and did the same, taking a bite from my sandwich.

"Just curious," I said as I took another bite an opened a bottle of root beer.

"Curious about what Billy?" Ron asked in a mild but decidedly testy tone.

"It is the prerogative of any prosecutor to revisit unresolved cases sometimes. Some things I thought should have been in the file were not there. But I am confused about the 20 questions from you. This could become an open case and I would be restricted from talking to you."

"Hey I asked because I wanted to know if you found anything that might shed some light of who killed him. George was also friend of mine, remember."

"I was just curious about some of the things that were not in the file that should have been there."

"Cool. What else is new? Are you adjusting ok?"

"There is not a lot to adjust to. The office pretty much runs itself. I figure that more than 90% of all the cases we handle are routine. Plus, you left me with a great staff. I am enjoying the experience so far."

"Good. Things are pretty hectic around here. Trying to change the status quo and make sure that basic city services continue to be delivered is going to take a while. The unions are pissed because of the 3% raise I am proposing in the budget. I have also proposed eliminating the automatic step increases and converting to a merit system. I might need your help in eliminating the patronage system. It would be good if you could announce that you support it."

"You should have asked me that before you announced your intentions to get rid of it. I rather like the idea of being able to clean house if I want to. That was the process you used to reorganize the DA's office when you first took over. I will have to think about it before I decide whether I will support the ending of the patronage system."

"Spoken like a true brother of the Lodge. That is the same answer I would have given."

"I learned from the best."

"As much as I would love to continue shooting the shit, I have an appointment at 1pm and it is that time now. Let me know if you find something about George."

I shook Ron's hand and walked out of his office. Outside in his waiting room were five nervous looking pale white boys with all kinds of maps and architectural drawings.

"Mr. Morgan, you are on time. You and your entourage have exactly 15 minutes to tell why you think I should change my decision not to support your project," Ron said winking at me as he escorted the group into his office.

Why was Ron concerned about my inquiry into the George Martin case? I could not get that question out of my head as I walked back to my office. Ron has never been known to make a casual inquiry about anything. Was it someone from the FBI who told him or was it from inside my office? Ron had sent me a letter requesting Mrs. Metcalf's transfer to his office. I decided on the way back to expedite that process. She was a good secretary, but her loyalty was to Ron and I needed my own secretary.

All the files and other information I had requested were on my desk when I returned. I chuckled to myself. Ron must have called Mrs. Metcalf and told her it was alright to let me have the files. Then I stopped, for I realized that his power was not to be underestimated.

The FBI transcripts of the surveillance conducted on the Syrians revealed very little about who could have possibly killed George. However, the transcripts did contain several conversations where the Syrians were complaining about the press and everyone accusing them of killing George Martin and Oscar Williamson. Ansur Thomas was quoted on the tape as saying, "Snake was with us, why in the fuck would we kill him? We had cut a deal with him for him to double cross that nigger Jackson. We got him on the hook. He fell in love with the white horse."

That explained George's erratic behavior, but it still did not give a clarify who killed him. Because my personal involvement in the case involved a potential conflict of interest, and because I needed confidentiality, I decided to hire someone who would be more objective to review the case.

That evening at dinner, I told Janice about Ron's reaction and she had the same response. However, she was more concerned with how he found out about it.

"You need to be careful. Ron hand-selected all the staff in the key positions in his office; they are all loyal to him first. Over time you are going to have to evaluate all of the people in your office from the custodian to the attorneys to weed out those who you don't trust."

"That will take some time to do. I think I am going to try to create a couple of new positions first. These will be people I will hire."

"Why do you think he is so concerned about your interest in George Martin's investigation?

"I don't know and I need to slow down because I might be overreacting to something that is not there."

"There can only be an upside to your looking at it; you might figure out who killed him. Remember the old saying, be careful what you wish for." Janice looked at me with those hazel eyes as she got up from the table and walked over to me and sat on my lap.

"Will is spending the night with his grandmother. I need to be rocked to sleep."

"Hmmm, that calls for a bottle of wine."

"At your service," Janice said as she got up and went in the kitchen and came back with two glasses and a bottle of white wine. "It is not Boone's Farm or Ripple. It is a French Chardonnay."

"I like the way you say French."

CHAPTER 19

More than four months had elapsed since I had hired Raymond Whitherspoon to do a preliminary review of the case.

I met Ray when I came home in 1968. We both took and passed the state bar exam at the same time. It was Ray's third try after having failed twice. Ray was from Chicago and had gone to night school at Rooselvelt University in Chicago. While waiting to pass the bar exam, Ray had worked as an investigator for the DA's office. He had hoped to be hired as an assistant DA after he passed the bar, but Johnson, the DA, thought otherwise. So, when Ron was elected I recommended he hire Ray. Ray worked for Ron for three years before deciding to quit and go into private practice. He now was the dope dealers' lawyer. The drug dealers used him because they figure if he was half as good at defending them as he was in prosecuting them, they had a good chance of avoiding jail time. Ray had been a defensive lineman in college and, unfortunately, he had not maintained any type of fitness regime since those days. His football playing size was 6'4, 230 pounds. He now lumbered around carrying at least an additional 120 pounds on that same frame. Two years ago. Ray had developed a form of Parkinson's disease that caused him to slur his speech. It had not however in anyway affected his legal intellect.

My initial reaction to his lack of response was that he was trying to run up his bill on me. But he squashed that when he sent his first invoice in for only 5 hours for three months worth of work. He indicated in his first invoice that he was having a problem that old.

I had just returned to my office from the downtown shopping mall looking for a birthday present for Janice and trying to get in some early Christmas shopping. I was told that Whitherspoon had been waiting almost two hours to talk to me. He was sitting in the outer office when I came in.

"Attorney Raymond Whitherspoon, it is so nice to see you. Is this a social visit or do you have something to report that will justify the huge sums of money the city is paying you?"

My comments left him speechless. He just smiled and shook his head and followed me into my office.

"Let's sit over here." I wanted him to sit in a chair at my small conference table as opposed to sitting on the couch. I kept visualizing him sitting on the couch and not being able to get up. Ray sat down and put his brown satchel on the table. He opened the satchel and took out a manila folder and put it on the table.

"I finally got a copy of the ballistic reports and compared them," Ray began. "What I found out prompted me to contact you immediately." He took out four pictures of four bullets. "These are pictures from three different shootings. This first one is the bullet that killed George Martin. The second one is the one that killed Oscar Williamson and the third is the one that killed Ansur Thomas."

"That's only three killings, you have four pictures."

"The fourth one is the picture of a bullet that killed a drug dealer and an innocent bystander in front of a bar four years ago. All four bullets were fired from the same weapon."

"Are you serious?" I stood up to get a better look.

"I am not only serious, but I have an 85-95 percent match."

184

"What made you match up these three with the one from the drug killings?"

"Just got lucky. The expert I use likes to use a blind test to test his accuracy. He just happened to select the ballistic test from the drug killings because the caliber of bullet was the same."

"Were you able to determine if there was any link between the drug killings and the other three?"

"The only connection we were able to make—and it is a stretch—is that the drug killings were the result of a turf battle between two drug dealing gangs. A real mean character named Teddy Chambers controlled one of the gangs. This Chambers guy and George Martin were childhood friends. Like I said, it is a stretch."

"Your stretching has revealed more than any of the FBI and police investigations could in seven years." I had to turn and walk toward the window to hide any facial expression I might have upon mentioning George's murder. "Have you developed any theory on why George was killed?"

"In the transcripts, there is an implication that George was hooked of heroin. I did not mention it because I cannot verify it. I thought maybe George did not pay his dealer, and the dealer either popped him or had him popped."

Taking all of this in my mind raced with the knowledge that T.C. was a sniper in the army. It was something I did not want to think about.

"This is where I am. I wanted to talk to you before proceeding. I think that the drug killing is the best potential lead, but the drug dealer is a good friend of the Mayor Jackson. I have some clients who I can talk to who might possibly shed some light on who the shooter was in that killing. Once I can identify a possible suspect in that killing, the door to this mystery starts to open."

"I agree. I want you to keep me informed on a more regular basis now. We need to talk at least once a week. This is some good work," I said as I fumbled through his files. "You also need to submit your vouchers on a more regular basis now."

"That's a bet," Ray grunted as he struggled to get up. Moving a 350 - pound hulk around was not easy. "I will call you next week."

We shook hands as I walked him to the door. I closed the door and sat down on the couch. This shit had T.C. written all over it. What I could not understand was why? The George Martin murder might be explainable if, in fact, George was using drugs. However, in the killing of Oscar Williams, Ron and Meat were also shot. T.C. would never risk harming them. I tried without success to rationalize that the ballistics evidence could just be a coincidence. Yet, the evidence suggested that T.C. was linked to at least one and possibly four murders. The Ansur Thomas connection was an additional puzzle. I now had a list of 20 questions to ask with no answers in sight. How did a shooter who may have been contracted to kill George Martin, a small level drug dealer from the South End, and a ward politician, also get a contract to kill the leader of organized crime in Petersville?

***

The pace of Christmas holidays were an ideal diversion for me. I was feeling a little pissed at Ray for dropping all of this shit on me three weeks before the holidays. Fortunately, the quality and quantity of holiday activities that an elected official is invited to participate in is overwhelming enough to take almost anything off your mind. This was my first holiday experience as the DA, which made it impossible for me to decide which events I needed to attend. So, I tried to attend all of them. What I soon found out was, except for a couple of rare instances, they all were essentially drunken food affairs. The goal of most of the party hosts was to get you to look and act just like them: overindulgent pigs and alcoholics.

One of the parties that Janice and I attended, which did not fit into this mold was the party Ron gave. It was his first party as Mayor and he went out of his way to make sure that everybody knew that there was a new sheriff in town. His first attention getting move was to have it at the South End Waiters' Club, in the heart of the black community. Ron did not spare any perk. He had valet parking and hostess's greeting people at the door to check your coat. I had bought Janice a Mink jacket for Christmas and gave it to here early. This was the first time she had worn it. When we got inside the club she was reluctant to give her coat to the hostess to check it.

"This is not a project party baby," I told her. "Plus, I got the coat insured. It is ok to check it."

She laughed, hesitated, then slowly pulled her coat off, looking at me through the corner of her eyes sending a clear message to me that she was doing it with reluctance.

Ron and Lyzette stood at the front entrance to the ballroom shaking hands and greeting people. As we stood in line to be greeted, a group was singing a very popular song by the Temptations called "Get Ready." The group had sung three Temptations songs by the time we got up to Ron and Lyzette.

"Merry Christmas brother," Janice and I said almost in unison. We exchanged hugs and kisses between the four of us.

"You and Janice are sitting with us at table one," Lyzette ordered.

"Is that Rondo's group up there?" I asked. Rondo was a group that did a Motown revue. They were hired to provide the music.

187

"Yes sir. And I told them you would be here and they had better learn some Temptation songs or don't show up." Ron said this while giving me a very broad smile.

Lyzette had prepared the food herself. She served up a menu of West Indian and Creole food that she was planning to include in a restaurant she planned to open soon in Old Town. It included a seafood gumbo, oxtails, fried and fresh oysters, jambalaya, and sweet tarts.

As good as the music and food were, Janice and I enjoyed watching the people even more. Especially the white elected officials and businessmen and their wives who had to come deep into the heart of the South End, some for the first time. It was mandatory attendance for some of the businessmen who were also sponsors of the event.

It took me at least twenty minutes to get to Ron's table with all the hellos, happy holidays and merry Christmases I had to say to people. I was still adjusting to all the superficial glad-handing I had to do because I was an elected official. Leonard and his wife Alice, Wiley and his date, and T.C. and Rita were at Ron's table. It was good to see all of us together for the holidays.

"The invitation said 7pm to 11pm. It is almost 10pm. Where have you guys been?" Leonard yelled out to us, as we were about to sit down.

"We have a child that we have to take care of. But it looks like we got here just in time. Don't tell me that you have been sitting here since 7pm?"

"Yes we have. And we have been celebrating. Wiley got the charter for his bank today."

"That is just great. When will I be able to open an account?" I said as I reached over to shake Wiley's hand.

188

"No later than July 1ˢᵗ. That's when I hope that the remodeling will be finished."

"I have never used a bank before, but I will change my habits for you," T.C. chorused in.

I made a deliberate effort to sit down next to T.C. at the table. He did not seem bothered by my sitting next to him, but then again, I couldn't remember a time when I ever saw him nervous.

"Hey Janice. What's up Billy? Or should I say top cop? How does it feel to be the top cop now?" T.C. asked me as I sat down.

I smiled and turned around to face him. I decided not to read anything into his comments and just answer his question at face value. "It is a challenge. I am coping. It is certainly a transition."

"Do you really like fucking niggers and putting them away?"

"Fucking niggers is not how I would describe it. In almost 99 percent of the cases I have sat in on, I thank God for prisons. Some of these 'brothers' have committed some horrible acts."

"There are also some cases that Billy has interceded in that have prevented innocent people from being prosecuted," Janice said in my defense.

"Stand by your man. I like that. I'm just fucking with you Billy. Somebody has to do the shit, and you will be fairer than most."

The band suddenly struck up a song by the Temptations that I had requested named "Ain't No Sun." It was off one of their early albums "Temptations with a Lot of Soul."

"Come on baby, let's bop," I said grabbing Janice's hand and pulling her up from her seat.

"Oh no, don't get him started, he will be talking about the Temptations all night now," Wiley said as I started toward the dance floor. He was right. I did not need a lot to get started talking about the Tempts.

"The greatest singing group. Ain't no sun," I sang as I started to swirl Janice around the dance floor. We stayed on the dance floor as the band and the group did a melody of Temptation songs. When I got back to the table, Ron and Lyzette had finally come over to sit down.

"You would stay up there all night if they kept singing the Tempts music," Ron laughed.

"I will never apologize for the admiration and respect I have for their talent," I responded.

"Let me borrow your husband for a minute. I need to ask him a business question," Ron said to Janice.

"That's all you got—a minute."

I got up and followed Ron to the bar. He ordered a Remy on the rocks for both of us.

"From my bottle," Ron told the bartender. The bartender reached up to the top shelf of his liquor cabinet and got a circular crystal- like bottle. The label on the bottle read Remy Martin XO.

"Private stock?"

"Lyzette's father turned me on to it when I was in Trinidad. I bought a couple of bottles when she and I went to the Seychelles. It is smooth as silk. You will like it."

It went down so smooth that it was scary. There was no bite to it at all. "Damn, this could sneak up on a nigger quick!"

"What did the ballistic test on the bullets show?"

"That was blunt question. Unfortunately, my answer is not going to be as direct. I can't tell you. You know that."

"Did it tell you who the shooter was?"

190

"We need to stop this conversation Ron. I will promise you one thing. I will let you be the first person I talk to before I release the finished report. How did you find out that the ballistic report was back anyway?"

"I have my sources."

"Ron, are you keeping tabs on me through an informant in my office?" Ron's head turned and his face had an irritated growl on it. He stopped short of responding at that exact moment. In a classic Ron Jackson self-deprecating tone of voice Ron apologetically answered.

"I am interested in this case for one reason and one reason only, to help you succeed."

Although I was unconvinced that his motives for spying on me were altruistic I let it drop.

"I will accept your explanation this time, but I want to tell you once more that I will not release anything about the investigation before talking to you."

"I am not worried about you Ron. It's your and my enemies who will try to use this investigation to embarrass us."

"Are you trying to tell me something? Because I cannot think of one thing happening as a result of this investigation that would be embarrassing to me."

"I just don't want any surprises. I am satisfied with your answer so let's get back to doing something important like listening to some music and dancing with our beautiful wives."

"I am going to have another glass of this cognac and take one back to Janice."

"Help yourself brother."

Ron walked away while I waited for the bartender to bring me another drink. Ron looked unusually disheveled when he was talking to me about the investigation. My head said it was strange, but my heart told me to dismiss it as part of his stress reaction to the new job. Whatever it was I was not going to let it spoil the night with my wife.

The band was supposed to stop playing at midnight, but Wiley gave them a $150 to keep playing for another hour. Billy Jr. was spending the night with his grandmother, so Janice and I had the night to ourselves and we made the best of it.

We got home at three o'clock and did not fall asleep until 5am. We took advantage this rare time by ourselves and proceeded to make passionate and loud sex without worrying about the pitter-patter of little feet walking into the room to sleep with us. It was a rare and not often experienced luxury. I had planned to sleep until at least 12 noon when I had to get up and go pick up Billy Jr. Unfortunately, the telephone interrupted that plan at 8:30. We decided to let it ring and not answer. It rang again at 8:35.

This time it rang 15 times before Janice shook me to wake me.

"Wake up and get the phone Billy. Whomever is calling is not going to stop until we answer and it is probably for you anyway."

"Shit. It's Saturday morning. If it is for me it had better be goddamn important."

"Hello!" I yelled into the phone.

"Mr. Strayhorn, this is Ray. I know it is early…"

"Early is the not the word, it is fucking early and this had better be fucking important!"

"I have got to see you immediately. I cannot talk to you on the phone."

"What are you scared of? And what is so important that it cannot wait until later in the day?"

"I am being followed. There is someone watching me as we speak."

"Where are you?" I asked, getting up to put my robe on.

"I am two blocks from your house at Ralph's Pancake House. You need to see and hear what I found out about Martin's murder."

"Shit Raymond are you sure we can't do this later?"

"Please, Mr. Strayhorn. I am becoming afraid for my life."

"I am on my way. Just stay in the restaurant." I hung up the telephone, got up and went over to the closet to get something to wear.

Ralph's Pancake house was a place where most of the late crowd ate breakfast after being up all night. It was only two blocks from my house. I looked out the window and saw the sun shining so I decided to walk. Ralph's was located in two refurbished railroad cars.

The temperature was in the mid-40's and the sun was shining. It only took me five minutes to get there. I walked into the restaurant and looked around for Raymond. One of the waitresses recognized me and asked if I wanted a table. Before I could respond, I heard loud noises coming from the rear of the restaurant. In the rear of the room I saw a man push open the men's restroom door with his shoulder. He began pointing and yelling at the manager behind the bar. I tiptoed up to get a better look.

"A man is in there bleeding all over the place," he yelled. He was sweating and breathing so hard the manager made him sit down. I went to the rear of the restaurant. I took out my badge, identified myself and told the manager to call an ambulance and the police. I saw immediately that it was Raymond. His throat had been cut. I checked his pulse. It was weak and he was barely breathing.

"Hold on Ray! An ambulance is on the way." In a very raspy voice he tried talking to me.

"Come closer," he said. I leaned over to get closer to hear him and he pulled me to his chest. "Post Office box 7878. It is all there."

"Don't talk Ray. You will be okay. Preserve your strength."

"Get...the key. It is...behind the...water tank."

I reached over and felt a key taped to the tank. Ray suddenly started choking. He then started falling. I could not hold him as he fell on the floor. I got on top on him to check his heart and could not pick up a heartbeat. I was still trying to talk to him when I felt someone pulling on me trying to get me off his chest.

"We will take over now Mr. Strayhorn," a voice behind me said.

Reluctantly I let them pull me up. The ambulance attendant immediately started working on his wound, trying to stop the bleeding. I slowly slipped the key in my pocket and backed out to give them some more room. The police were right behind them. They were talking to the manager who was pointing at me. One of them stayed at the front door to keep people from leaving while the other officer walked briskly towards me.

"Mr. Strayhorn, I am officer Sanders. Do you know what happened?"

"I was supposed to meet the victim, Ray Whitherspoon, here for breakfast. When I walked into the restaurant, someone from the rear of the restaurant started yelling that a man had been cut. I walked back there and found Ray sitting on the commode bleeding profusely from the throat area. I tried to talk to him but I

194

could not understand anything he was saying." Just as Sanders was about to ask another question, two other men walked up behind him."

"We will take over now officer," a short five feet wide by five feet tall nattily dressed white officer said. "Mr. Strayhorn, I am Detective Barstow and this is Detective Osborn."

"We are from homicide," Osborne said. He reached out and shook my hand. "You want to go into the manager's office to talk? It will be less of a circus atmosphere."

"I agree."

"Officer Sanders. I want you to interview every soul that was in here when this happened. That means *everybody*. And nobody leaves until I say so." Barstow continued to give Sanders additional instructions while he and I walked over to manager.

"We need to use your office." The restaurant manager handed Barstow the keys and pointed us to the other side of the restaurant. The people in the restaurant were getting antsy and started giving the uniformed officers a hard time, questioning them about when they were going to be able to leave. I stopped and picked up a glass and knife and started hitting it to get their attention.

"For those of you who don't know me, I am District Attorney William Strayhorn. A man has been brutally stabbed and maybe dead. The police will have to conduct a thorough interview with each person that was here when the incident happened. Including me. We all have something else to do, including me, but I will also have to stay to be interviewed. If you cooperate it will be over before you know it. Please have a little patience so that the officers can do their job. Thank you." I put the glass down and continued walking back to the office.

"The was very good Mr. Strayhorn. It is rare to hear a public official support us," Osborne said.

I had to think of a quick story to tell them. Under no circumstances would I tell them what Ray and I were supposed to talk about. That would be just like calling the Gazette and sending them a press release. The restaurant manager's office was more like a closet than an office. It was also the place where cleaning supplies were kept. Osborne sat in a chair behind the desk while I sat in a chair in front of the desk. He took off his coat and took a note pad out of his pocket. Osborne looked like he was about 35. He had sandy red hair and sky-blue eyes. He opened the note pad and started asking questions.

"You knew the victim?"

"Yes his name was Raymond Whitherspoon. I was here to talk to him about a job at the DA's office. He had worked there before as a staff attorney about three years ago."

"He was an Attorney?"

"Yes."

"Who's idea was it to meet here?"

"It was his idea."

"Do you know of anyone who might want to kill him?"

"No, I don't."

"Is this the same Whitherspoon that handles the cases for the drug dealers?"

"The same. He told me he was getting tired of private practice and wanted to come back to the other side." I saw the opening I needed to direct the investigation towards Whitherspoon's drug clients. The questioning continued for another thirty minutes. Osborne then thanked me for my patience and I went home.

It was almost noon and Janice was frantic until I told her what had happened. However, I did not tell her about the key.

"Who do you think did it?"

"I can only surmise it was whoever he thought was following him."

"You might need to be careful honey. If these people have already killed six people, killing seven will not bother them."

"I am going to get a police chauffeur next week."

"I told momma I would pick up Billy Jr. at noon and it is 12:30 now. I think we need to get going." I nodded in agreement and we left to go and pick Billy Jr. Checking out the contents of that post office box would have to wait until later.

CHAPTER 20

The key said, "Main Post Office." I assumed the key was to a post office box at the main post office located on Madison Avenue on the edge of downtown Petersville. Since the post office box area is open 24 hours, I waited until after 6pm to go and see what, if anything, was in the box. By now I had begun to get a little paranoid, so I left home driving in the opposite direction of where I was going to see if anyone was following me. If anyone was following me, they were good because I did not see anyone. I got there at about seven-thirty and found a parking space right in front of the building. Box 7878 was in the right corner of the box section.

Walking through the cavernous empty lobby of the Post Office, I tried to calm myself by remembering that no one knew about the key except me. I walked around to the other side to see if anyone was following me. There was not a soul in the place, so I walked back to the side where box 7878 was and stuck the key in, turned it, and held my breath. I stooped over to look inside. There was a thick manila envelope pressed inside the box. I pulled it out and quickly locked the boxed. I walked briskly back to the front entrance of the building, trying to look as inconspicuously as I could to avoid looking nervous.

I got in my car and drove straight home. I parked in front of my house and again I looked around to see if anyone had followed me. It was a little past 8pm when I finally walked into my house. Janice was still up giving Billy a bath.

"Ron called. He said call him whenever you get in. He will be up awhile. A detective Osborne also called. He said you could call him tomorrow. I cooked some chicken and made a salad." By the time she had finished talking, I had walked to the back of the house and was standing near the bathroom door.

"Daddy!" Billy yelled.

Janice turned her head and looked up. "Why did you let me continue to yell when you were standing there?" she said with a glad to see you anyway smile.

"I just like hearing your voice. I will eat later. I got to read a file before I go to bed."

"On a Saturday night? Tomorrow is Sunday baby."

"I know but this cannot wait."

"Does it involve what happened today?"

"I cannot talk about it right now. It is confidential and…"

"Don't say it, you know I know not to say anything."

"I'm sorry honey. Seeing Ray's body slumped over, bleeding, and his neck slit has upset me."

"I do understand. Just make sure you don't forget to eat."

I walked into the bathroom to get Billy out of the water. Kissed Janice on her cheek and walked downstairs to the basement to a makeshift office I had assembled. It had a desk, an IBM typewriter and a phone. I took the folder from under my coat and sat it on the desk. I put my coat on the back my chair and sat down. I don't know how long I had been sitting there staring at the envelope when I heard Janice knocking of the basement door.

"Billy, pick up the phone. Didn't you hear it ringing? It's Ron." I had slipped into such a deep trance that I did not hear the telephone.

"Okay Janice, I got it. Hello?"

"I am truly sorry to hear about Ray. He was a solid guy and a damn good trial lawyer," Ron offered. "Are you okay?"

"Thanks for calling, I am fine."

"What happened? All I know is what I read in the police report."

"I don't know. He called and said he needed to meet with me to discuss the case. When I got to Ralph's he had been cut open and was bleeding to death."

"You did not get a chance to talk to him?"

"No, he was dead when I got there." The phone suddenly went silent.

"Ron...are you still there?"

"Yes, I, uh, was looking at something on TV. Well, hang in there and stay tough. Wait, I almost forgot the other reason I called. I want you to co-chair a juvenile crime task force for me. It will be you and a minister."

"Let me think about it and get back to you."

"Okay. I'll call you later on in the week."

"Yeah, later."

I hung up the telephone and again stared at the manila envelope. It had tape wrapped around it that I slowly began to peel off. I moved around in my chair to get comfortable. Inside the envelope was a hand-written document labeled *"George Martin et al."* The penmanship of the author was clear and concise. Unlike my own handwriting, I had no problem reading this.

Ray had discovered some interesting coincidences that had led him to conclude that T.C. was the shooter in at least one of the murders, and perhaps all of them. One of his clients had actually told him that T.C. was the shooter in the murder of the drug dealer. This fact, combined with the ballistic information alone, could implicate him as the shooter in the other five shootings.

The client that gave Ray this file was doing life in a state prison. He had also told Ray that the rifle used was one that T.C. still owned.

Ray conducted a series of interviews with witnesses who identified someone who looked like T.C. on the scene of George's murder as well as the shooting and murder incidents involving Ron, Meat, and Oscar Williams. I had been sitting for two hours when the phone started ringing and forced me to get up.

"Mr. Strayhorn, I am sorry to call so late. I thought you might want to know that we think we have a good lead on who might have killed Attorney Whitherspoon."

"That would be extremely good police work detective. Who is this person?"

"His name is Anthony Saleem. He is a cousin of Albert Saleem. He was seen following Mr. Whitherspoon into the restroom right before he was killed. We are looking for him now. Several of the patrons at the restaurants picked his mug shot out of our files. We have an all-points bulletin out for his arrest. I will call you when I get any additional information."

"Thank you, Detective. I appreciate the call."

I hung up the phone and started thinking that maybe I was wrong. I might have jumped to a conclusion too soon. Reality will always bring you back, which is what the ballistic test kept doing. It was late and I had told Janice that I would go to church with her tomorrow. I had been promising for a month of Sundays that I would go with her and little Billy. Her father was giving the sermon and with all I had on my mind, this would be a great Sunday to go.

Bishop Jackson's sermon made me feel better. He talked about taking responsibility for your own actions. It helped me to let go of the burden I had put on myself regarding the murders. I was worrying so much that I was going to need therapy.

"I did not kill anybody so stop worrying," I told myself. "I did not drop anything so there was nothing for me to pick up."

After church Janice and I went to her parents' house for dinner. At dinner her father told us that the church had finally given him his new assignment. He would be the Bishop for a diocese in Africa.

"I did not know that the AME still had a presence in Africa," I told him after hearing where he was being assigned.

"A large and active church and missionary effort that is growing," the Bishop responded.

"Well, I guess we will just have to pack our bags and go with you," I mused. "Billy Jr. and Janice and I will not be able to survive without you. We cannot just let anyone keep him." Everyone laughed as I got up to get another piece of cake. "Y'all can laugh all you want. I am serious."

"We won't be leaving until next year sometime. You will have plenty of time to get used to it."

"Maybe you can just take Billy Jr. with you."

"Oh no you don't," Janice said as she elbowed me in the side.

"Just kidding, just kidding."

"I read in the paper where one of your colleagues was viciously murdered yesterday. Were you and he close?" the Bishop asked.

"Not really. I hired him to do some legal work for the DA's office. I knew him professionally but not personally. As much as I am enjoying the company, I have got to go home. I have a full and early schedule tomorrow morning. I need to get home and do some reading."

"We do understand," the Bishop said.

We got home right in time to catch the local evening news. The telephone started to ring almost at the same time that I turned on the TV. The news was showing a scene of a body being taken out of an apartment building. The reporter was describing the incident as I was answering the phone.

"Hello."

"Mr. Strayhorn, this is Detective Osborne. Are you watching the news?"

"Yes."

"Damn, I have been calling all afternoon. I had hoped that I could talk to you before the news came on. We found Saleem."

"Was that Saleem in the body bag?"

"Yeah, that's him. It looks like a suicide. We have not finished our investigation yet, but we found a rifle and some shells. We have sent them to the lab for a powder burn and ballistics analysis. We also found what looks like a suicide/confession note. The press does not know about it yet. I thought you might want to see it."

"Where are you?"

"I am downtown at police headquarters."

"I will be there in 15 minutes." I hung the phone and grabbed my coat.

"Janice, I have got to run downtown to police headquarters. A suspect in the Whitherspoon case has been found dead. It looks like a suicide. He left a note that the investigating officer thinks I need to see."

"Don't be too late."

"I won't."

I got to the police station in ten minutes. It was normally a 15-minute drive at the speed limit, but I was pumped. I tried to calm myself as I approached the building. My thoughts went back to the only other time I had been in this building. It was 1962, and Ron and I were in the holdover cell waiting to be bailed out. We had been arrested for trespassing at a downtown department store during a demonstration to get them to hire blacks as sales clerks. That seemed like a lifetime ago, but it was only 12 years. Now Ron was Mayor and I was the DA. Detective Osborne was waiting at the front door to escort me in. This allowed me to avoid having to identify myself and be subjected to a search. I was becoming more and more impressed with Osborne. Most of the white policemen I encountered reacted to me with a smug arrogance. Osborne was respectful.

He escorted me to the elevator where we got in and he punched number seven. The lobby was full of people being either processed in or processed out. The seventh floor was where the homicide offices were located. Osborne was dressed casually--a contrast to his normal suit and tie appearance.

"Is Sunday a casual dress day for the homicide division?" I asked.

204

"Only for those who are not working with the public. This is normally my off day. The duty officer called me when they found Saleem." Osborne directed me to a conference room in the middle of the homicide area.

"I will go and get Lt. Huber," he said, showing me to a chair while he walked over to an adjacent office.

He returned to the conference room accompanied by a uniformed policeman who was the epitome of bubba from the "Police Academy" movies. He was at least 6'4 and weighed more than 300 pounds.

"Mr. Strayhorn, it is a pleasure make your acquaintance," he said in a slow drawl. "I'm Lt. Warren Huber."

He sat down next to me in a chair that looked like he had spent some time in because seat sagged just enough to fit his huge ass.

"This Saleem killing looks like it will close a lot of open files." He gave me a two-page type written note enclosed in a plastic sleeve. "Our boy Saleem has confessed to killing everyone except JFK."

I read the letter and Huber was almost right. The letter said Saleem was a hit man for the Syrian mob and that he had killed more than 25 people, but he only listed ten. Included in that ten were George Martin, Oscar Williams, Ansur Thomas, Raymond Whitherspoon and some drug dealer named Eddie Thomas. It was all neatly packaged.

"You and the Mayor were personally involved in the Oscar Williams murder, right Mr. Strayhorn?" Huber asked, interrupting my train of thought.

"Yes, I was. But I don't think we were the targets."

"This is all preliminary. We won't be able to verify anything until we get the ballistics analysis back."

"You might not have to do one. Whitherspoon did one on the bullets that killed Martin, Thomas, Williamson and the drug dealer. He has an 85% match. I can get the report to you tomorrow morning. I understand the motive for killing Ray, but what I can't figure out is why he would now kill himself."

"That is all we have to go by right now. Oh, by the way, he was clutching this patch when we found him." Osborne passed to me what I immediately recognized as a Special Forces patch.

"That is a Special Forces patch. They were the craziest or bravest soldiers I ever encountered in my life," Osborne commented.

I nodded my head in agreement, remembering a time when my unit had to do a tactical parachute jump with a Special Forces unit at Ft. Bragg, North Carolina. They played all kinds of practical jokes that were not funny to us. They would unhook your static line and hand it to you or give you one that might be an extra one as you were about to jump. Real scary motherfuckers.

Suddenly I remembered where I had seen a patch like that before. It was on T.C.'s arm when I saw him at Ton Son Nhut airport in Saigon. I made myself a mental note to check and see if T.C. and Saleem were assigned together at any time.

"I am going to leave it open until after the autopsy is complete and the ballistics analysis is re-checked and the rifle is also checked out. Call me if you find out anything."

It was almost 9pm when I got home. I decided to pass on reading the file and went straight to bed. I was not able to get any sleep. Anxiety over the factors surrounding Saleem's death kept me from sleeping. I got up at 5:30am to get the earliest edition of the Gazette that I could. The suicide note had not been released so I figured that I had about one day before the story would break. Although I dreaded what I might find out about these murders, I had to pursue it. I had to know—it was my job to find out the truth.

I left for work early, so I could get there before anyone else. The office did not officially open until eight. A quick check of T.C.'s army record showed that he and Saleem were in the same unit in the Special Forces. They did a tour of duty in Vietnam together. After confirming their military connection, I understood why Saleem was clutching the insignia. I thought it was going to be hard for me to make a decision about what to do, but it wasn't. I called Ron and told him to come by and pick me up in his car. He responded without question as if he was expecting my call.

I told my secretary that I had a meeting outside the office and I did not know when I would return. Ron was waiting for me in front of the Courts building.

"Just tell Meat to drive to a secluded spot."

Ron told him to drive down by the old coal yards near the river. For the first time in our lives both Meat and I saw Ron nervous. His nickname was "never nervous" Ron, but he was sweating bullets. When we got to the river, I motioned for Meat to stay in the car.

"We are going to walk around for a minute," I told Meat as I opened the door. Ron got out on the other side.

"What's up?" he said with a nervous grin that could not hide his fear.

"I want to tell you a story about a group of young, gifted, black boys growing up in the slums of a major industrial city in the U.S. Notwithstanding their social status in neo-slavery America, they had dreams. One of them (in particular) had the wildest dream of all. He dreamed and believed he could become the mayor of their hometown. Most of his friends, except for one of them, thought he was a little crazy. He ignored the naysayers

207

and completed college—he even got a law degree. He convinced his best friend to go to Law school with him and they both graduated together. One of their friends was the nephew and adopted son of the most powerful black politician in the state. When his friend's uncle died suddenly of a heart attack, his mother passes on the mantle to him. The nephew asks his closest childhood friend to work with him on his campaign. My ambitious friend saw this as an opportunity to get a jump-start into politics. He was promised a seat on the city council if he helped him run his campaign. Unbeknownst to him, his political friend was a junkie. The nephew had cut a deal with the Syrians to appoint someone the Syrians approved of to the city council instead of keeping his promise to his friend. When the ambitious friend discovers the double cross, he is furious. So furious that he has his good friend murdered by another childhood friend.

After his friend dies, the mother of the dead friend appoints him as replacement Democratic Committeeman. He subsequently is elected District Attorney and again is faced with an ally who decides to double cross him and join up with the Syrians. This time, he conceives an even more diabolical plan. He stages an assassination attempt on his own life. He has his friend (who was a veteran of the U.S. Army Special Forces unit and an expert marksman) wound him and his bodyguard while killing his rival. This makes him a martyr--a hero in the black community. But our guy decides he needs a permanent solution to the problem of the Syrians who are extremely reluctant to give up the influence and power that derives from their control of the political apparatus on the South End. So, our guy comes up with a plan to neutralize the Syrians.

He learns from the FBI that the Syrian families are feuding over how the loot is being divided and our friend decides to use this feud to instigate further internal feuding among the Syrian families. He has his sharp shooting friend kill the patriarch of the Syrian family and makes it look like one of the rival families did it. An all-out war breaks out, which eliminates his main political opposition. Our friend wins re-election as DA and then sets his sights on the Mayor's office. He achieves his dream then appoints his friend to replace him as DA because he believes he will have someone there who will watch his back. He is also scared to death that one day someone will find out what he has done.

But the friend that he gets appointed DA decides to review the unsolved murder of George Martin. He hires a lawyer who quickly starts to uncover circumstantial evidence that points at the real shooter. The lawyer is killed and the shooter stages the suicide of a Syrian friend of his to deflect the attention away from him. However, he does not plan on the guy leaving a confession suicide note, nor does he expect him to leave a clue that the DA is able to trace back to the real shooter.

And now the DA has this dilemma. Does he turn in his friends whom he has known all his life? Or does he just ignore what happened? The decision is really easy. He cannot turn in his friend. But all he needs from his friend is one answer to one question: "Did you kill George?"

"No, I did not," Ron answered straight-faced and swift.

I took a manila envelope from my briefcase and laid it on the ground. I took a can of lighter fluid and book of matches from my briefcase. I sprayed the envelope with lighter fluid and then struck a match and lit it. We both stood there and watched it burn. When it had burned completely, I kicked the ashes and put my arms around Ron. I started walking back to the car. Ron was still standing there, looking at the ashes. I yelled over my shoulder to Ron.

"T.C. needs to disappear for a while, until the heat recedes. You can handle that?" I turned in time to see Ron shaking his head to indicate that he could. "Then let's get some lunch."

Virvus Jones

Follow me on Facebook & Twitter

facebook.com/virvus.jones

Twitter **@VirvusJ**

COMING SOON

The Stalking Horse II

The stakes are even higher for District Attorney Billy Strayhorn and Mayor Ron Jackson as they navigate Petersville politics.

Ready to self-publish your book?

vozwritingpartners@gmail.com